EDDIE COLLINS' INVESTIGATION INTO THREATENING LETTERS BEING SENT TO HIS A-LIST DIRECTOR FRIEND MIKE FORD TURNS UP MURDER, RAPE, KIDNAPPING, REVENGE.

What Collins finds points to people involved in the filming of a movie Ford directed years ago called *Red Desert*. A rape was committed during that shoot, and Eddie begins to believe that the wrong person may have been convicted of the crime. Two deranged actors, seeking revenge, kidnap his daughter and hold her in a remote canyon. When wildfires threaten to engulf the entire region, the attempt to rescue her is jeopardized and Eddie's long-time friendship with Mike Ford is tested, a friendship forged against the backdrop of Hollywood, where friends and loyalties come and go like shifting sands.

"My friend Clive Rosengren has created a guy I'd like to get to know: Eddie Collins. I wouldn't mess with him, but you'd want his number in your wallet."—*Tom Hanks*

"I like this character Eddie Collins. He's tough, funny and has the classic private eye's world-weary wisdom. I hope to see much more of him."—*Michael Connelly*

"Kidnapping! Murder! Wild fires! Hollywood veteran Eddie Collins tackles it all in his latest outing. Veteran insider, author Clive Rosengren, swings a wide net for his actor-cum-private eye. Collins adeptly switches from actor to P.I., follows clues, soothes emotions and solves several crimes. Enjoyable, fast and loaded with the author's trademark keen insights."—*Carl Brookins, author of the Sean P.I. series.*

RED DESERT

Clive Rosengren

Moonshine Cove Publishing, LLC
Abbeville, South Carolina U.S.A.

This book is a work of fiction. Names, characters, places and incidents are products of the author's imagination or are used fictitiously. Any resemblance to actual events, locales or persons, living or dead, is entirely coincidental.

ISBN: 978-1-937327-58-3
Library of Congress Control Number: 2014960053
Copyright 2015 by Clive Rosengren

Book interior and cover design by Moonshine Cove staff; cover image public domain.

Acknowledgments

Once again, thanks to the members of Monday Mayhem for nurturing this book through its development: Carole Beers, Michael Niemann, Sharon Dean, and Tim Wohlforth.

Thanks also to my early readers for their notes, comments and suggestions: Sue Lyon, Karen Olson, Holmes Osborne, Chris Peterson, Sarah Phelan, Kathy Rosengren, Larry Rosengren, and Brad Whitmore.

ALSO BY CLIVE ROSENGREN

Murder Unscripted

ABOUT THE AUTHOR

CLIVE ROSENGREN spent the better part of the last forty years as an actor before turning to crime fiction with his debut novel *Murder Unscripted*. Featuring Hollywood actor/private eye Eddie Collins, the book was nominated for the Best First PI Novel by the Private Eye Writers of America. *Red Desert* marks the second appearance of Hollywood sleuth Eddie Collins. Rosengren spent eighteen of those forty years in Hollywood, where he pounded many of the same streets as his fictional detective. He appeared onstage at the Great Lakes Shakespeare Festival, the Guthrie Theatre, and the Oregon Shakespeare Festival, among others. His movie credits include *Ed Wood, Soapdish, Cobb, Bugsy,* and *Three Fugitives*. Among numerous television credits are *Seinfeld, Home Improvement, Ellen,* and *Cheers,* where he played the only person to have thrown Sam Malone out of his own bar. He is an avid movie fan, and has a collection of over one thousand titles, including all the Oscar-winning films and performances. He lives in southern Oregon's Rogue Valley, far away from the hurly-burly that is Hollywood.

Visit him at his website cliverosengren.com.

RED DESERT

Chapter One

Janice Ebersole knew she shouldn't be swimming bare-assed naked. Not to mention having another glass of wine. But there she was. The long-stemmed goblet was partially full, perched on the edge of the pool under the diving board. The glass picked up dancing reflections from the swirling water. The night was hot. Except for a few strategic spotlights, the backyard was dark.

The boutique's air conditioning had broken down, giving Janice an unexpected night off. She'd hoped to spend it with Mike, but he had some stupid symposium he had to attend. He invited her, but she didn't want to go. Boring. They'd had a little spat. He'd told her to go to his place, use the pool, and he'd be home as soon as he could. She'd walked to work, so Angie dropped her off. She had a key to his house. At first she'd been pissed, but when she looked at the pool and felt the heat, she finally said to hell with it, opened a bottle of his most expensive Chardonnay and decided to cool off.

She scissor-kicked her way the length of the pool, raven hair splayed out like a watery Medusa. She glided to the deep edge. One hand clasped the concrete drainage gutter, her other elbow slung over the edge. She reached for the glass, tilted it up, swallowed the contents and placed it back on the cement deck. She paddled to the ladder on her right, found the bottom step and pulled herself from the pool, lights from the bottom glinting off her supple body. She picked up the empty glass and filled it from the bottle sitting on a glass-topped table. Her cell phone lay on a towel. She picked it up. No messages. A boom box played some light rock from a CD. She kicked up the volume a notch, sipped some wine, and began dancing to the music, droplets of water from her black mane of hair peppering the cement.

After another sip, she climbed the ladder on the diving board and walked toward the end. Then she started to lose her balance. She giggled and sat down, looked around. A slight breeze ruffled the fronds of the palm trees surrounding the pool. She could smell forest fires burning. Her eyes became heavy. She lay back along the diving board. Maybe a little nap would refresh her. She didn't want Mike to think she'd drunk too much.

She didn't know that she was being watched.

***

The heat was stifling, not the kind of weather to be dressed in black, wearing a windbreaker that didn't breathe and a woolen watch cap. If you planned on breaking into someone's house, however, the wardrobe was appropriate.

As he strode up Nottingham Avenue, sweat broke out on his chest. He could see the faint glow from the forest fires burning to the northeast. The acrid smell of wood smoke drifted through the Hollywood Hills. Crickets chirped off to his right in the deep brush. In the distance, the lonely bark of a dog filled the night air. He'd encountered no one on his trek up the incline. Streetlights were spaced approximately fifty yards from each other, providing little illumination.

The house appeared on his left. He was certain the occupant was gone. Ford was leading a symposium at the American Film Institute. *The Hollywood Reporter* had run the story. The girlfriend worked nights and didn't live with him. Just to be sure the house was vacant, he crept up to the garage and peered through the small window in the door. Empty. An enclosed corridor led to the front door of the residence. He hugged the wall as he made his way to the main entrance. The security company's name was embossed on a small metal stake piercing the lawn next to the sidewalk. Good advertising for the company, but an easy means of access to their website. He'd googled them and had easily hacked into their system. The schematics and passwords followed.

Off to the right side of the front door a six-foot high wooden gate led to the rear of the house. It was locked of course. No problem. There had been no indication of any form of motion sensors. He grabbed the top of the gate and vaulted over, dropping soundlessly to the cobblestone walkway. He'd cased the house for weeks and had never seen a dog of any kind. And now he heard no warning growl or bark.

What he did hear, though, was the sound of music coming from the backyard. This was unexpected. The house was supposed to be empty. The intruder snaked his way through a stand of hydrangea along the side of the house. The aroma mixed with night blooming jasmine, temporarily erasing the smell of wood smoke. He approached a sliding glass door. His fanny pack contained a glass cutter and rubber suction cup. Would he need them? He peered through the door. The room was empty. He gently pulled on the door handle. It was unlocked. Was someone in the backyard?

He crept toward the end of the house and saw her. She danced on the cement next to a diving board. Floodlights from the bottom of a swimming pool caressed the curves of her naked body. Nice, he thought. Very nice. And posing a problem. Would he have to subdue her? Would she disappear into the house?

The intruder watched as she refilled a wine glass from a bottle sitting on a nearby table. After looking at a cell phone, she raised the volume on a portable disc player, danced briefly, and climbed the ladder to the diving board. She teetered to the end, almost losing her balance. He heard her laugh as she sat down on the board, then lay back. He stared at her for several moments, her arms extended over the edge of the board. She was silent and still.

Time to move. He reversed his tracks and carefully slid open the glass door. He squeezed through and looked around the room, getting his bearings. To his right, another glass door, this one wide open, looking out onto the pool. Two small table lamps provided the only illumination. A huge stone fireplace, open on both sides, dominated the space. On his left a wall of shelves spanned the room. Floor to ceiling. They were filled with books, pictures, knickknacks, and what looked like trophies. Glancing back toward the pool, he approached the shelves and briefly looked at the snapshots, then the trophies.

There it was. Nestled among several statuettes. Some of the others were more ornate, but this was the one he wanted. Thirteen and a half inches high, twenty-four carat gold-plated, a knight standing on a reel of film, grasping a crusader's sword. For decades the figure had been called Oscar. The film spool had five spokes, one for each of the original branches of the Academy.

A perfect place for the envelope. He pulled a square of black velvet from a pocket of his windbreaker and unfolded it. A gloved hand reached up and plucked Oscar from his perch. He wrapped the statuette in the cloth and dropped it in an inside pocket. From another he pulled out a letter-sized envelope and placed it where Oscar had sat, leaning it against an adjacent small glass obelisk. Glued across the face of the envelope, in cut-out letters that looked like a child's handiwork were the words "Mike Ford."

A framed snapshot caught his eye. He leaned in for a closer look. Ford with a young girl in his arms. Standing next to them was a man sprouting a full beard and wearing one of those porkpie hats. The front gate of Disneyland was silhouetted behind them. The intruder lifted the photo from the shelf and dropped it in another pocket.

"What the hell are you doing?"

He whipped around to see the woman standing in the open glass door. A large bath towel covered her nakedness. He started moving toward her.

She retreated through the door, backing toward the

pool. "Stay the fuck away from me. I'm calling the police."

She lunged for the cell phone lying next to the open bottle of wine. Before she could punch a key, he grabbed her, wrenched the phone from her with his left hand. The towel dropped to the cement. He wrestled her to edge of the pool. Her fists pummeled him. She began to scream. The water made her body slippery against the vinyl of his windbreaker. She started to get away. He grabbed her from behind, left arm around her throat. The screaming became garbled. She furiously kicked, drawing them both to the edge of the pool. He slipped on a puddle of water, almost losing his balance. The arm around her throat loosened and she screamed again. He pulled the statuette from his pocket and pounded the base end of it down on her right temple. The screaming stopped. Her body sagged. He let go of her and she fell. With a sickening thud, her forehead struck the edge of the pool. Her head snapped back and she slipped into the water. The intruder watched as she slowly sank. The body bounced off the concrete bottom of the pool, then it came to rest, on its back, arms and legs spread-eagled.

He put the Oscar back in his pocket, knelt and looked at the body. No flailing of arms and legs. No motion whatsoever. He looked around. No sounds. She hadn't been heard. He got to his feet and placed the cell phone on the table next to the wine bottle. He darted toward the side entrance of the house. A quick glance over the top of the gate revealed an empty street. The intruder lifted the iron latch, slowly pushed the portal open a crack, slipped through and softly closed it behind him. He removed his gloves, windbreaker and watch cap as he strolled down the street, just another neighbor out for an evening walk.

Back at the swimming pool, the woman's body gently swayed with the movement of the water. It eerily drifted to the surface, bobbed for a moment, then rolled over. Her dark hair floated in all directions around her head, a black stain in the water.

On the glass-topped table the CD stopped playing. The cell phone began to chirp. It rang five times. Then it was silent.

Chapter Two

Mickey Patterson's breath smelled like two-day-old egg salad. That, combined with an overpowering dose of Old Spice and his acne-scarred face thrust into mine was making me nervous and nauseous. He had me pressed up against a fake wall. A stage brace poked me in the back. He was once again giving me directions.

"You gotta give me air, Eddie, plenty of air."

"I'll give you air, Mickey."

"No, I mean, you really gotta give me air. Sometimes these live audiences don't pick up on the cue. Especially if your line is off-camera. So you gotta give me air. Hold for the laugh."

He was close enough to me that a few droplets of saliva splattered against my pristine cop uniform, causing me to further dislike the little twerp. This dislike had started almost from the moment I had shown up on the set at the start of the week. It was a Friday night and we were minutes away from the final taping of a sitcom called *Before the Beginning*. The studio was full. I was playing Officer Danforth. Mickey's character, Benny Bonnano, had been arrested and was waiting for his buddy, Percy Shank, to come and bail him out.

Just as I was again wondering what in the hell I was doing here, a bell sounded. Cameras were ready to roll.

"Remember, Eddie, air, plenty of air. All right?"

I pushed myself away from the protruding stage brace and leaned into the face full of acne.

"Listen, pal. I know you've been doing this for a lot of years, but so have I. Gimme a break, man. You know how this works. You get the laugh, Mickey, I'll hold for it. Now get the hell away from me."

The assistant stage manager, Jack Abrams, had been listening. Out of the corner of my eye I could see him shaking his head and laughing. He tapped Mickey on the shoulder.

"Come on, we're at places for scene seven. On set please."

Mickey backed up, a hurt look on his face, his eyes as big as saucers.

"Well, sheesh, Collins, you don't have to get so defensive. I'm just trying to do the best show we can."

He actually seemed to be pouting as he walked through a door onto the set, which was in fact the interior of a police precinct.

Mickey Patterson and his co-star Denny Stinson had a modest hit on their hands with this sitcom. They'd been picked up for their fourth season, and had just learned that they'd also gotten the "back nine," an extension of nine episodes beyond the network's original order of thirteen.

Patterson wasn't a novice. His career started when he was a kid, submerged for a few years, and now had taken off again with this show. Given the fact that he'd been around for a number of years, you'd have thought he would know how to deal with a fellow professional. I have little patience for actors like this who think they know it all simply because they got their SAG card before their driver's license.

Tony Cantone, this episode's director, was an old friend of mine. He'd brought me in to play Officer Danforth without having to go through the menial audition process, where one smiles artificially and says how much one has enjoyed watching the show. The truth is I'd never seen *Before the Beginning*, but I wasn't about to tell anyone that. Morrie Howard, my agent, had negotiated "top of show" for me, which meant I was making a pretty good piece of change and had decent billing, something other than "man in leisure suit" or "florid bartender." The fact is I must have charmed someone because they had written me into a second episode, shooting next week. More of the Mickster.

Jack walked up and handed me a paper towel. "He's a piece of work, ain't he?"

"I'm cancelling my membership in his fan club."

I swiped at the front of my uniform, trying to erase the evidence of Mickey's plea to not step on his laugh. Jack motioned me over to a video monitor, then handed me a microphone and I waited for my cue from Benny Bonnano.

An actor playing their attorney was getting both ears full from the two co-stars. Mickey received his setup, delivered the line, and bingo, got the laugh. I waited until it ebbed, said my off-camera line, and double bingo, garnered an even bigger response than the Mickster. Jack giggled and punched me on the shoulder.

Say hello to the pro from Dover, Mickey.

***

The taping went well, despite having to reshoot one of Benny Bonnano's scenes several times. Apparently there was a camera snafu, but it also became obvious that Mickey, the comic genius, kept blowing a couple of lines. When the cast took its bow in front of the studio audience, he caught my eye and gave me a wink, cocksure that he had just given me a lesson in Comedy 101.

Tony Cantone caught up with me on my way to the dressing room. He was a small man with a shock of jet-black hair that looked like it could use the business end of a hairbrush. Our paths had crossed several times over the years. I was glad to see that he was landing gigs fairly often.

He stuck out his hand. "Good working with you again, Eddie. Been too long."

"That it has, Tony."

"And you're in again next week, right?"

"I am. You directing it?"

"Nope. I've got to put this one together. Andy Willis is on deck."

I started unbuttoning my shirt and looked over my shoulder to see if I was being overheard.

"How the hell do you manage to work with that Patterson kid? Doesn't he drive you nuts?"

Tony nodded and ruffled his mop of hair. "He's a pain in the ass, I know. But the suits love him and the network wins their time slot, so—"

"—He could be Jack the Ripper and it wouldn't make

any difference," I said.

"That's about it." We laughed and shook our heads, both of us all too aware of actors rising to their level of incompetence in this business called Hollywood. "Hey, someone told me you opened a detective agency. True?"

"Collins Investigations. Smack dab on Hollywood Boulevard."

"No kidding? So, what, you do it as a hobby or something?"

"Well, tell you the truth, Tony, what I just got done doing here is turning out to be more the hobby."

"I hear you. It's a young man's town."

"Unless you're Jack the Ripper."

"I guess. So what kind of stuff do you handle?"

"Nothing too serious. Divorce, bail jumpers, stuff like that."

"Nothing juicy? Like murder, or something?"

"Once," I replied, thinking back to several months ago when my life had been turned upside down for a few weeks. "But I think I'll leave that to the cops."

"So, if I'm doing a project with a private eye in it and need a consultant, you're the one to call, right?"

"You could do that. You could also give me a buzz when you need someone to play the PI. I've had some experience."

"You got it."

We traded business cards and again shook hands. I headed for the dressing room, pulling off my uniform shirt as quickly as I could.

***

Darkness had descended during my confinement on the Disney lot. It was still hot. A bloodshot moon hovered over Burbank. The air was pungent with the smell of smoke from fires burning in the hills, a yearly occurrence. I started walking along Mickey Mouse Lane toward the parking structure, then took a right onto Daffy Duck Drive. Uncle Walt still loomed over the Mouse House. All the studio streets offered homage to the Disney pantheon. I had a brief fantasy of some middle-aged accountant suddenly snapping and flitting around the lot doing the appropriate cartoon voice on every street he landed. Maybe there's a sitcom there.

I stopped under a streetlight, pushed my porkpie back on my head, and pulled out my cell phone. The contraption and I still weren't all that compatible. My secretary Mavis was doing her best to remove me from the roster of Luddites, but it was slow going. I had become somewhat familiar with the fool thing clutched in my hand, but right now, standing under the streetlight, I was stymied in my efforts to check for messages.

I heard footsteps behind me and turned to see Sarah Dowling coming toward me. She was in the cast of *Before the Beginning*. A pretty little strawberry blonde. We had shared a couple of pleasant conversations over the lunch table. She made me wish I was ten years younger.

"Hi, Mr. Collins. Sorry I missed you after we wrapped. I wanted to tell you I really enjoyed working with you."

"Right back at you, Sarah."

She walked into the light and brought with her the faint trace of a very fragrant perfume.

"How much do you know about cell phones?"

She set her tote bag on the ground. "What's the problem?"

"I'm trying to access my messages. Think I've run aground here somehow."

"Let me have a look." She took the phone from my grasp. "Scroll down to voicemail, then punch this button."

"Aha, I see. I was punching that one."

"That turns it off." She pushed another button and showed me the phone. "There you go. Nothing in your mailbox."

"Good. I'm not sure I'd know what to do if there was."

She laughed and picked up her tote bag. "Do you tweet?"

"Do I what?"

"You know, twitter, text? With your phone?"

"You just saw the extent of my expertise. I'll have to leave twittering to the birds."

She giggled again and we continued to the parking structure, making small talk about show biz. I saw her to her car and wished her good luck down the road.

My Cutlass was one level up. I crawled in, turned it over and opened the windows. The raspy sounds of Tom Waits emanated from the speakers with "Warm Beer and Cold Women" from *Nighthawks at the Diner*. Wonder if Waits tweeted? With that voice, probably not. I felt like I was traveling down a gravel road as the veteran troubadour took me along Riverside, then Barham across the freeway and into Hollywood.

Chapter Three

The building's elevator lumbered to my floor. The door creaked open to reveal Lenny Daye, one of my neighbors. He's the major domo behind *Pecs and Abs,* a magazine featuring pectorals and abdominals of the masculine persuasion.

"Eddie, honey, how the hell are you?"

"Hangin' in there, Lenny. Just got off a shoot."

"Be still my heart. The actor lives. Tell, tell."

"A sitcom. *Before the Beginning.* Ever heard of it?"

"That thing with Mickey Patterson? Sweetie, I could tell you stories that would make you blush."

"I'm sure you could."

Lenny was usually a walking display of sartorial splendor. Tonight was no exception. A jaunty beret sat perched on his head. He wore a black turtleneck with a single strand of gold chain draped around his neck. A black vest complimented the turtleneck. Skin-tight black leather trousers were tucked into knee-high boots.

"Looking sharp, Lenny. Very Beat, Greenwich Village, that sort of thing."

"Thanks, dearie. I'm hoping to get my bongos thumped tonight."

"Yeah, well, take care of yourself."

"Yes, mother." He smirked and strutted into the elevator, blowing me a kiss as the door slid shut.

Always a highlight of my day, running into Lenny. A Russian doctor and a modeling agency were my other neighbors. The former I knew very little about and the clients going in and out of the latter were winsome and willowy, definitely not who Lenny had in mind when it came to getting his bongos thumped.

I slid home the dead bolt in the front door. Mavis leaves her desk lamp on for me. And she scatters Post-It notes. One told me she would be coming into the office tomorrow. Some mailing needed to be done.

A second square of yellow paper stuck to the phone informed me I needed to call Helen Boylston in the morning. Helen had hired me a few days ago to look for her husband, Jack, who had disappeared. They'd been married for fifty-something years and Jack had started to show some signs of mild dementia. He'd been a studio contract player years ago, appearing in most of the early television shows and countless numbers of movies. Helen was devoted to him and very distraught when he didn't come home one day. She'd found me through a mutual actor friend. I'd managed to locate Jack after a couple of days. Seems as though he'd gone to visit Jimmy Whitmore, a buddy of his from some oater they'd worked on. Both of them got a little juiced up swapping yarns, and Jack just decided to stay for a couple of days. I guess he kind of forgot he was married. I found him sitting on the beach, flirting with a couple of volleyball bunnies and making a fool out of himself.

Next to the phone sat the answering machine. It was blinking and held one message, from Morrie Howard, asking how the shoot went and telling me to call him on Monday morning. I hadn't yet told my agent that I now had a cell phone, primarily because I'd have to program another number into the damn thing.

Filling a chair in front of my secretary's desk was a cardboard box. Mavis buys and sells antiques and collectables on the internet. Collins Investigations isn't exactly floundering, but the number of cases I handle is small enough to necessitate her devoting herself to another endeavor on the side. And she does pretty well. Consequently, I never know what oddities will greet me.

I folded back the cardboard flaps and saw two smaller boxes inside. A plaster gnome about nine inches in height was inside one. I didn't know if Mavis was leaving me a message, but the gnome was mooning me. In the other box was its companion. This one had his pants down around his knees and was squatting in preparation for...well, you get the picture. Where she gets these gems is beyond me. And who actually buys them is an even greater mystery.

I walked into my office and found some mail on the desk. Bills, mostly, save for today's edition of *The Hollywood Reporter* and two residuals. The net total of both would buy me a steak dinner, providing it was a cheap cut and I didn't order any booze or dessert.

A doorway draped with beads separates my office from my living quarters. As I walked through the strands, I was engulfed by the heat that remained in the studio apartment from the day's sunlight beating through the south-facing windows. I hit the light switch and one for the ceiling fan, peeled off my shirt, then opened the French doors overlooking Hollywood Boulevard. I turned on a large floor fan and put it in front of the windows. So much for air conditioning.

I punched the remote and flipped the television to a Dodgers game. They were losing to the Giants. I grabbed a beer from the mini-fridge and filled a glass with Mr. Beam to keep it company. After cobbling together a pastrami sandwich, I put it and a bag of chips on a footstool and picked up the copy of the *Reporter* and leafed through it. I certainly don't pretend to have my pulse on the Hollywood scene, but I try and keep up with who's doing what to whom in the biz.

As I took a bite of the sandwich, my eye caught a story on one of the inside pages. The headline read, *Woman Found Dead in Swimming Pool*

The story went on to say that Janice Ebersole, girlfriend of Mike Ford, had been discovered nude, floating in the actor's Los Feliz swimming pool. It had happened last night. Police said preliminary investigation was inconclusive. The victim apparently had slipped and struck her head on the edge of the pool. Death appeared to be from drowning.

My sandwich sat untouched in front of me. The story hit home. I knew Mike Ford. We had worked together years ago doing summer stock. Both of us had subsequently come to Hollywood, albeit a few years apart. We'd remained good friends, catching ball games together and enjoying the occasional poker night. He'd even provided me with employment a time or two over the years. Only a month ago he'd invited me along on a trip to Magic Mountain with his daughter and Janice.

I picked up the remote and channel-surfed until I saw local news footage on the story. On the screen Mike was seen leaving his house on Nottingham and crawling into a black SUV. Reporters hounded him, but he had nothing to say. I was stunned. Mike was a great guy and a fine actor. He'd been handed a couple of good breaks and had capitalized on them to the point where he now commanded top dollar. He'd also gone on to direct some of his pictures. His success as an actor had even garnered a handful of awards, the most noteworthy being the little golden guy called Oscar.

The reporter tossed the story back to the studio and they went to a commercial, another irritating shot of a couple sitting in separate bathtubs gazing into a sunset.

I nibbled on the pastrami sandwich. It tasted like Play-Doh. I sipped my beer and absentmindedly surfed through a few channels, finally landing on Turner Classic Movies. All of a sudden coincidence exploded from the screen. There in front of me was William Holden floating face down in a swimming pool. The scene was from Billy Wilder's classic *Sunset Boulevard*. Norma Desmond's delusion eventually led to the demise of Holden's Joe Gillis.

As I listened to Holden's voice-over, the similarities between reel and real life came cascading into my head. Art imitating reality? Not quite. Unlike Norma Desmond, I was certain Mike Ford hadn't lost his senses. But what he had lost was a girlfriend.

Chapter Four

Two floor fans were turned up high. All they succeeded in doing was to blow hot air around the cramped, squalid apartment. The space was a converted garage behind his landlord's house. Small windows, one of them filled with a worthless a/c unit. Bathroom, one tiny bedroom, sofa, kitchenette, the bare essentials. For years he'd been promising himself someplace else to live. The low rent always dissuaded him.

A TV sat next to a large dining table, which served as his desk. He ate his meals off a cigarette burn-scarred coffee table. A laptop and printer/fax/copier took up most of the bigger table. The rest of it was cluttered with paste, scissors, newspapers and periodicals.

He sipped from a bottle of Rolling Rock and took a hit off a corncob pipe full of brand new green bud. After a moment, he let loose a cloud of smoke and rubbed the cold bottle of beer across his forehead, then leaned back into the sofa. Television news footage showed Mike Ford being hounded by reporters as he made his way to a black SUV.

He stared at the television set. Last night had been a disaster. The woman caught him completely by surprise. He'd panicked, but it couldn't be helped. She would have identified him. The only comfort he had was that he was certain he hadn't left any trace of his presence at Ford's house. The news coverage said nothing about the possibility of the woman being a murder victim. They were saying she'd drowned. He wasn't sure, but he thought he'd hit the woman's head in the same spot where she'd connected with the edge of the pool. The statuette had been wrapped in velvet. Would it have left a mark?

The Oscar sat on the corner of the coffee table. He picked it up and again wrapped it in the cloth, then tapped the base of it on his bare thigh. No mark. A second blow, this one a little harder. Still no noticeable trace. Fuck it. He wasn't going to worry about it. He'd covered his tracks, left no evidence.

His cell phone rang. He picked it up and checked the caller ID. Jimmy Whitmore. He'd been expecting the call.

"Yo, Jimmy, what's up?"

"What's up with you, Hal? Christ, I saw the news. What happened?"

"Ford's girlfriend was there. I didn't expect that."

"They said she drowned. Did you do it?"

"She was gonna call the cops. I hit her with the Oscar. Knocked her out. She slipped and fell in the pool."

"Oh, man, this fucks up everything."

"Jimmy, relax. I didn't leave any prints. I can't be traced to last night."

"But now the cops are involved, big time."

"So what? They won't have a suspect."

"They'll be snooping around Ford like stink on shit, Hal. Maybe we should hold off on this thing for a couple weeks."

"Jimmy, listen to me. We've gotten Ford's attention with the two letters. We have to follow through. The woman's drowning might be a good thing."

"How the hell can you say that?"

"It'll make him realize that someone's after him and that they're damn serious."

Hal listened to the silence on the other end of the line as he sipped his beer. Finally Jimmy said, "I don't know, man. I ain't got a good feeling."

"It'll be all right," Hal replied. "Trust me. Did you get the key from Boylston?"

"I got it. Made a copy."

"Good. I'll meet you tomorrow at that little dive on Ocean. Just south of the Pier."

"Chez Jay?"

"That's the one. With the good breakfast burrito."

"I'll be there. Later, man."

Hal broke the connection and took another hit off the pipe. He glanced at the Oscar in front of him. It looked good in the room. A splash of gold. Gave him cause to fantasize. What could have happened if he'd gotten the breaks, right? As a kid he remembered watching the ceremony and imagining being up there in front of millions, making an acceptance speech and thanking all the little people. Yeah, well, maybe in another life. He picked up the cold bottle of beer and finished off its contents.

Jimmy's waffling was unsettling. Hal would have to work on him some more. Ford had to have read the two letters by now. Using the title of the Patterson kid's show in the first one was inspired. Put the suspicion on someone else. Stealing the Oscar and leaving the second note was going to fuck with Ford's mind, make him skittish. The woman's death was a snag, but it happened, so be it. Move on.

Hal went into the kitchen and pulled another Rolling Rock from the fridge. He set the bottle on the coffee table and picked up a DVD laying next to the TV. A Mike Ford title. One of the earlier ones. Some dumb-ass thriller taking place in South America. He sometimes wondered why the hell he continued to punish himself by watching these damn things. But they fueled the flame, kept the resentment, stirred the hatred.

The film started. Hal took another hit off the pipe and settled back into the sofa. The screen filled with the image of Mike Ford, a face he'd gotten to know all too well. The face of a betrayer.

Chapter Five

I watched Marilyn Monroe and Charlie Chaplin duck into Starbucks for a cuppa joe. Only in Hollywood. They are but two of filmdom's faux icons that hang out daily around Graumann's Chinese Theatre, which now, to the tune of five billion dollars, is known as TCL Chinese Theatre. The corporate plunder of Tinseltown continues unchecked.

One of the many pleasures of my life is to stand on my mini-balcony and watch Hollywood Boulevard come to life below me. I stood sipping my morning coffee as Marilyn and Charlie came out with their brews and headed back to the theatre, where they would pose for pictures and receive small gratuities in exchange for their chutzpah. Marilyn was in her *Seven Year Itch* white frock and Charlie, of course, was the Little Tramp. They bounced and minced along, stopping periodically to satisfy an already burgeoning onrush of tourists.

I finished my coffee and went back inside, closing the French doors and drapes in anticipation of the day's heat. Local television news was providing more details on the fires. Two of them were raging in the San Gabriel Mountains above La Crescenta. A spokesman for the firefighters was optimistic they could be contained in the next couple of days. Provided the winds died down. Those, of course, would be the Santa Anas, the much-heralded hot, dry gales that sweep through the Los Angeles Basin from the Mojave Desert. With no rain, they can easily fan infernos throughout the hills.

I refilled my coffee cup and heard the morning anchor switch to the Mike Ford story. LAPD was now saying that someone besides Janice Ebersole may have been at the scene of the accident. Ford's Oscar was missing. The police weren't saying if the disappearance of the statuette was linked to the death of the woman. It was an ongoing investigation.

As I sat watching the news story, I heard the arrival of Mavis in the outer office. After a moment, she knocked on the wall next to the beaded curtain.

"Permission to enter the lair?"

"Permission granted."

She pushed through the beaded curtain and came in. As usual, Mavis brought an always-welcome brightness into Collins Investigations. Red was the color *du jour*, a fine compliment to her blond hair.

"Did you see that story about Mike Ford?"

"Yeah." I pointed to the TV. "It's on right now."

She moved behind me and we watched shots of Ford in front of his house.

"Have you seen him lately?"

"About a month ago."

"Did you know his girlfriend?"

"I did. Nice lady."

"Very sad. An accident, right?"

"Well, now the cops are saying they're not sure. Mike's Oscar is missing. Somebody else could have been there."

We watched in silence for a moment until the story ended.

"You better give him a call, Eddie."

"I'll try to reach him this afternoon."

She walked over to the French doors. "Are you going to leave these closed?"

Mavis invariably feels the need to get fresh air into my apartment. Sometimes her efforts make me feel like I'm living in Death Valley.

"I am. If I need fresh air, I'll go to the movies." I switched off the television. "By the way, are you sending me some sort of message?"

"What do you mean?"

"Your two little plastered friends in the cardboard box?"

She thought for a moment. "Oh, the gnomes! Aren't they adorable? A lady down in Long Beach wants them."

"You going to repackage them before they go to Long Beach?"

"Eddie, what in the world are you talking about?"

"One of them was mooning me, for crissakes!"

"Oops." She giggled and put her hand to her mouth. "I forgot. Yes, I shall rearrange the little dears. Just for you." She headed for the beaded curtain as I picked up my porkpie and followed her. "How did your shoot go yesterday?"

"Fine, despite Mickey Patterson."

"What's the matter with him?"

"He's not funny."

"I've seen him on that show. He made me laugh."

"Yeah, well, there's no accounting for taste."

She slapped me on the arm as I sat behind my desk. "Don't forget to call Helen Boylston."

"What did she want? Jack take off again?"

"I don't know. She didn't say."

"I can't keep running out there all the time."

"It's Venice, Eddie. By the ocean. Cooler than it's going to be here."

I looked at her and saw the grin on her face. "That's the best idea you're going to have all day."

"Except for the one about Mickey Patterson being funny."

I shook my head and picked up the phone as she disappeared into her office. Helen didn't want to reveal what the problem was. She'd tell me when she saw me. I hung up and wrote checks for a couple of bills, an agent's commission being one of them. Which reminded me to give Morrie Howard a call. No need to wait until Monday morning.

Mavis appeared in the doorway and made an elaborate show of putting a bubble-wrapped gnome into its cardboard box. I gave her a thumbs-up as Morrie's tape came on. I told him I was sending him some money and that the sitcom was going well. He'd be pleased to know that his client was making him proud.

When I walked into the front office, Mavis was sealing up the box containing the bare-assed gnomes. I handed her the bills and asked her to mail them. She set them next to the gnome box on her postage scale, which sat atop a small cabinet in a nook off the front office. A bathroom, sink, coffee pot and God knows what else fill the space. I long ago had had my head handed to me for rummaging around in there looking for something. I don't think I've crossed the threshold since.

I slapped my porkpie on my head and headed for the door. "See you later, kiddo."

Mavis stuck her head out of the nook. "You keep that cell phone of yours turned on, don't you?"

"I do."

"Remember you've got to keep it charged."

"Got it plugged into the cigarette lighter. That how you do it?"

"That's how you do it. Just don't forget it when you get out of the car."

I snapped to attention and flipped her a salute. "Roger that, ma'am."

She rolled her eyes, but then grinned. "I'm very proud of you, Eddie. And pretty soon you're going to know your way around the computer."

"One step at a time, Miss Microsoft."

I shut the door behind me and walked to the elevator. A long and lean client of the Elite Talent Agency was waiting for the car, punching keys on the cell phone in her hand. She looked up as I approached.

"Good morning. You're Mr. Collins, aren't you?"

"Eddie. And you are?"

She offered her hand and I took it. Long fingers, firm grip. "I'm Jill Norton. Are you really a private detective?"

"I am."

"Kool." She pushed more buttons and the elevator door opened. I watched her for a moment as we lumbered to the main floor. Curiosity got the best of me.

"Are you twittering or texting?"

"Tweeting. I'm telling a friend of mine I'm in an elevator with a real-life private eye."

"I'm flattered."

She laughed and punched more buttons. The elevator door opened and we stepped out. "Nice to meet you, Jill."

"Same here, Eddie." She turned to go and said, "My friend says I should hire you."

"You need a private eye?"

"I might. One never knows these days."

"Well, you know where I am."

She smiled and walked towards the street. I watched her, wistfully, I must admit, then made my way to the rear door of the building. Maybe I should have Mavis explain this tweeting and texting business.

Then again, maybe I should just act my age.

Chapter Six

Venice is a funky little community. Abbot Kinney, a tobacco millionaire, founded it back in 1905. He had canals dug in hopes of recreating its Italian namesake. I think he fell short. Scrunched between Los Angeles, Santa Monica and Marina Del Ray, the community is home to a cross-section of residents, poets, artists, beach people. Back in the fifties the Beats thumped their bongos. Real ones, not those my neighbor Lenny Daye had in mind. Then the sixties gave rise to the hippies. Jim Morrison hooked up with Ray Manzarek here and gave birth to The Doors. Julia Roberts flashes her smile in Venice. Dennis Hopper lived here. Even Jeff Bridges' memorable character "The Dude" from *The Big Lebowski* had his pad in Venice.

Many of the streets are very narrow, accommodating only pedestrian traffic. I walked down one of these, only a block long. A breeze blowing in off the ocean made the air significantly cooler than the concrete of Hollywood. Small bungalows lined each side of the street. Jack and Helen Boylston's house had a cyclone fence surrounding a tiny front yard. A lemon tree with ample fruit occupied most of the lawn on the left side of a cracked and buckling sidewalk leading to the front door.

Helen answered my knock on the screen door. She was small and round in black slacks and a pale blue blouse. A thin gray sweater draped around her shoulders. Her wrinkled oval face lit up in a big smile when she saw me.

"Oh, Mr. Collins. Such a sweetheart to come all the way out here. In, in." I pulled the screen open and stepped inside. A small living room greeted me, chock-full of knickknacks. Small pictures adorned the walls. From my previous visit I remembered they were mementos of a lifetime in front of the camera.

"Jack disappear again?"

"Yesterday afternoon, but then he came home this morning. I feel so embarrassed calling you."

"No problem. I'm just glad he's back. Where did he go this time?"

She grabbed me by the elbow and steered me toward the rear of the house. "I made some fresh lemonade. Come sit. He's in the back watching one of his movies. The old fool." She shook her head. "He didn't tell me where he went. Jimmy said he didn't see him." She pulled out a handkerchief tucked in the sleeve of her sweater and blew her nose. "You'd almost think he's seeing another woman or something." She chortled and yelled through the doorway of a little den. "Jack, Eddie Collins is here. Turn that thing off!" She reached into a cupboard and pulled down three glasses. "Go in there and try and talk some sense to the old goat."

I walked through the door. He was sitting in a battered recliner, a TV remote lying on his chest. A movie that wasn't immediately recognizable to me blared from a set on the other side of the room. An open DVD case sat on top. Next to the recliner was a sofa with a coffee table in front of it. Magazines were strewn across it, among them *TV Guide* and *The Hollywood Reporter*.

Jack Boylston was a short man, lean and wiry. Wispy brown hair still grew on most of his head. His face was lined with wrinkles. A thin moustache spread across his upper lip. He had slippers on his feet and wore baggy jeans and a faded brown cardigan sweater.

"Hey, Jack."

He jumped when he heard my voice and turned to me. "Collins? Jesus Christ, you 'bout scared the shit out of me!" He pushed down the foot rest of the chair and paused the DVD.

I picked up the case from the TV set and immediately recognized what Jack was watching. "You were in this?"

"Yeah."

"With Steve McQueen?"

"That his name?" He snorted and waved his hand in dismissal. "Guy had a fuckin' chip on his shoulder."

"Steve McQueen. I'm impressed, Jack."

"You wouldn't be when you see the residuals they send me. Couldn't buy a pot to piss in with 'em." He took off one of his slippers and scratched the bottom of his foot. "What the hell you doin' here? Come to rescue me?"

"I hear you took off again yesterday."

"Went for a walk. Lost track of time."

"Helen said you didn't come home last night."

"Ah, she don't know what the hell she's talkin' about. I'm here, ain't I?"

"But you weren't last night. Where did you go?"

He ran a hand through his sparse hair and looked out

the window. "I'm not sure. I probably went over to see Jimmy."

"You talking about Jimmy Whitmore?"

"Who else? Unless he's using his stage name. Whit...Whit something or other. I forget."

"Helen told me Jimmy didn't see you."

"Well, sometimes he don't know what the hell he's talkin' 'bout either."

Helen entered bearing a tray with three glasses of lemonade and a small plate of cookies on it. She leaned over to place it on the coffee table.

"Move those papers, would you, Mr. Collins?"

The death of Mike Ford's girlfriend was one of the front page stories in *The Hollywood Reporter*. As Helen set the tray on the table, I held the paper out toward Jack.

"Did you see this? About Mike Ford?"

Jack snatched it from my hand and squinted at the paper.

"Yeah, serves him right."

"Why do you say that?"

"I worked with him one time. He starred in the damn thing. Directed it too. Treated me like shit."

"Oh, pish, be quiet," Helen said. She handed me a glass of lemonade and the plate with peanut butter cookies on it. "These are fresh yesterday." I took one and she handed the plate and a glass of lemonade to her husband. He grabbed one and sat back in his chair. I nodded my thanks and sipped the lemonade. "What did Mike Ford do to you, Jack?"

"Like dirt. Treated me like dirt."

"Jack, for Pete's sake, the man lost his girlfriend. Show some respect," Helen said. She sat next to me on the sofa.

"Never showed me any." Jack bit off a chunk of cookie and swiped at the crumbs that fell on his sweater. "Thought he was God Almighty on the set."

"Well, he was the director," I said.

"Don't mean he has to act like his farts don't stink."

"Jack, such a potty mouth!" Helen let out a deep sigh and shook her head.

I tasted a cookie and said, "What was the name of the picture?"

"Ah, I don't know. Red sunset..red dawn...red something. Out in the Mojave. Hotter'n a hundred-dollar hooker." He chewed on his cookie and stared off into space.

I turned to Helen. A sad little smile formed at the corners of her mouth. She rolled her eyes, then said, "Didn't I hear that his Academy Award was stolen too?"

"Yes, it was," I said.

Jack erupted with a mouthful of cookie crumbs. "Good! Never should have won it in the first place. Knew where he lived, I'd a taken the damn thing myself."

"Jack, you're just terrible." Helen pulled her handkerchief from under her sleeve and wiped her nose.

I drank some lemonade and set my glass on the coffee table. "Jack, you can't keep wandering off like this. One of these times something bad is going to happen to you."

He chewed for a moment and looked at me. "Little excitement in my life wouldn't hurt."

"True enough. But not that kind. It's not fair to Helen.

She worries about you."

"Don't have to worry 'bout me. I can take care of myself." He picked up the remote and restarted the DVD. The conversation had come to an end.

I finished my lemonade and stood. Helen did the same and we moved toward the door. I clapped him on the shoulder as I walked by him.

"Don't go off by yourself anymore, Jack. Take Helen along on your walks. Okay?"

"Yeah, yeah," he said. "Stay out of the heat."

Helen followed me to the front door. I opened the screen and turned to her. "Has he seen a doctor lately?"

"I have to practically tie him up and take him. I'm almost afraid of what his doctor will say. They might want to put him in a home. I don't know if I could deal with that." She again pulled out the handkerchief and dabbed at the tears that had formed at the corners of her eyes. "And I know he'd raise holy hell."

"Where does this Jimmy Whitmore live?"

"Not far. Over on Mildred."

"Does Jack ever drive over there?"

"Oh, good Lord, no. I won't let him drive anymore. I hid the car keys. We've got a little house up in Kagel Canyon. One day he said he wanted to drive up there and check on things. No dice, I said."

"Good thinking, Helen. Does Jimmy call you when Jack shows up?"

"I'm not even sure he knows Jack's married."

I wrapped an arm around her shoulder and gave it a squeeze. "Well, all the more reason to go along and introduce yourself."

She chuckled. "I guess."

"Does he work anymore?"

"Jack? Oh, no. He can't remember dialogue."

I nodded. "No, I don't suppose." I gave her another hug. "Maybe his doctor can talk to him." She nodded and I stepped outside.

"Thanks, Mr. Collins. I'm sorry to bother you."

"Call me Eddie, Helen. You take care of yourself. And him too."

"I'll try." She stepped back and closed the door.

I turned and walked to the front gate. Two young kids with skateboards were practicing in the middle of the street. One of them tried to jump the curb and fell flat on his ass. His companion had no sympathy for him and stood over him, taunting the kid.

"Treated me like dirt," Jack Boylston had said in reference to Mike Ford. I was surprised by the comment. I'd never heard that Ford had that kind of reputation. From what I was able to observe, Mike was well-liked by everyone who worked with him. He was one of the good guys in the business. I know actors who have worked with him as a director. None of them had expressed to me the opinion just voiced by Jack.

I turned the corner and headed to my car. It looked as though Jack was harboring some bitterness about his career having passed him by. And being unable to do much about it. Not unusual. Resentment was easily embraced by actors, especially by those who have been forgotten and live only with the past. Memories are to be cherished. Jack's seemed to have turned sour on him. I wondered if he'd had any contact with Ford since they'd worked on that film years ago. If he did, what had prompted it? Jack had said he didn't know where Ford lived. That ruled out the possibility of him showing up and making off with a gold statuette. Or did it?

Chapter Seven

The ocean always mesmerizes me. Maybe it's because I'm a Pisces. I sat in the shade of a palm tree on a metal bench at the corner of Ocean Avenue and Broadway in Santa Monica. The question running through my mind was why I haven't moved out here to escape the sweltering concrete of Hollywood Boulevard. I suppose it comes down to cost. A rule of thumb is the closer you live to the water the more you fork out in rent. I'd be busted if I pulled up stakes and found new digs out here.

But in the meantime the onshore breeze was cool and intoxicating. I was avoiding the drive back into Hollywood. Earlier I'd strolled out onto the pier and had a Dixie Fishwich at the Bubba Gump Shrimp Company. According to the menu, Forrest and Lieutenant Dan had one every day. A good enough endorsement for me.

People watching is one of my favorite pastimes. And I wasn't disappointed. It was Saturday. Everybody was out partaking of the California miracle, from skaters to joggers to just plain walkers. Santa Monica's homeless were also in attendance. A delegation of four of them sat on the grass, gazing about, choosing the targets for their panhandling skills. They passed a cigarette around. I was downwind of them. For their sakes, I was glad to detect that the smoke emanating from their powwow wasn't a controlled substance.

I lapped at an ice cream cone and watched an elderly couple slowly walk past me. Their hands were clasped together. The scene made me flash back to Jack and Helen Boylston. I didn't know the couple all that well, but I must say I was surprised at Jack's bitterness. I found it puzzling that he said he would have stolen Ford's Oscar if he only knew where Mike lived. It was difficult for me to believe that. At the same time, I couldn't help wonder what had prompted him to speak ill of the movie star. This vitriol from Jack didn't make any sense.

I also found myself wondering why I was taking such an interest in the Boylston's well-being. Something to do with respect for a fellow actor, perhaps. Jack was a survivor, one who had managed to string together a lengthy career in a profession notorious for treating talented people like second-class citizens. Deep down inside me there was admiration for a guy who had managed to withstand the Hollywood buzz saw. I sure wished, though, that he'd pay better attention to the woman who'd been at his side through all the years.

From my right a homeless guy approached and sat on a bench next to mine. His age was hard to determine beneath a sizable beard and long stringy hair that hadn't seen the inside of a shower stall in many moons. Beat-up sneakers covered his feet. He wore soiled cargo pants and an equally distressed gray sweatshirt. A couple of frayed sweaters completed the ensemble. A crumpled Dodgers baseball cap was pulled down low on his brow.

He looked at me for a moment and then nodded. "How are you today, sir?"

"Can't complain," I replied.

"No, that would certainly be counter productive on such a fine day as this." He looked over his shoulder, then moved to the other end of his bench. "You wouldn't happen to have any spare change, would you?"

There it was. The eternal question from one of his ilk. I turned to the guy. "What are you going to spend it on?"

"Nourishment. A sandwich. I have a great fondness for a Big Mac or a Whopper."

Normally I don't help these guys out, my reasoning being that it's like giving a potato chip to a seagull. All of a sudden you're fighting them off like mosquitoes. I'm also usually loath to give money to them because I think it will only aid and abet a drinking or drug problem.

It must have been the serenity of the ocean. The cool breeze. Something. I tossed the stub of my ice cream cone in a trash basket, reached in my pocket, separated a five spot from my money clip and handed it to him.

"Do me a favor. Savor every bite of that Big Mac or Whopper. And get some fries, too. Lots of ketchup."

He looked at the bill. "Alas, Mr. Lincoln here might not cover all that, sir."

He had me. I fished out another Abe and handed it to him. "No booze. Deal?"

"No, sir. Thank you. God bless you, sir." He got up, stuffed the bills into a pocket, and lumbered off across Ocean Avenue, on his way to a solitary banquet.

The elderly couple again walked in front of me, going the other direction. The old guy nodded and I did likewise. I watched them walk south where another homeless man approached them. The old gent politely shook his head and skirted around the panhandler. The guy stood in the middle of the sidewalk, talking to himself, looking out at the ocean. Then he spotted me and began to amble in my direction.

An orange woolen stocking cap covered his head. He had several weeks worth of stubble on his face. An Army field jacket was slung over one shoulder. He wore a long-sleeved denim shirt and wrinkled, dirty jeans.

He got about ten feet away from me and then froze, his eyes locked with mine. He stared at me for a long moment and then abruptly retraced his steps, walking backwards until he collided with a man who had a backpack slung over one shoulder. The guy yelled something and shoved him. The homeless man pounded on the walk sign as he continued to watch me, shifting his weight from one foot to the other. Finally he got the green light and disappeared across the street and down Broadway toward Santa Monica Place.

I stared after him, caught up in the oddness of this little encounter. The look on the homeless guy's face when he saw me was as if he knew me. And the strange thing is I thought I recognized him. I didn't have the faintest idea from where or when, but his face struck a chord in some back corner of my memory. I sat for a moment, trying to place him. I couldn't. Our paths had crossed. But where?

Chapter Eight

Hal was running late. The goddamn freeways again. Based on how Jimmy sounded over the phone last night, Hal suspected his tardiness was going to put him on edge. He wasn't wrong. As he walked through the front door of Chez Jay, he spotted Jimmy at a table, nervously doing a drum solo with a knife .

Hal shook his head as he plopped his backpack on a chair and sat down. He looked at Jimmy and opened one of the two menus in front of them.

"Sorry I'm late."

"No problem. Took a while to get a table."

"Fuckin' traffic. I was on the 405 for almost an hour."

"You outta move out here."

"With these rents? Forget about it."

"Aw, you can find someplace cheap if you look hard enough. Cooler out here too."

"Yeah, I'll grant you that. Goddamn Valley is the pits." A waitress drifted up to their table and Hal turned to Jimmy. "You order?"

"Nah. Just had a few peanuts."

Hal scanned the menu and looked up at their server. "I'll do a breakfast burrito. You have Rolling Rock?"

"Sorry."

He pointed to the draft sitting in front of Jimmy. "One of those will do."

She nodded and turned to Jimmy. "For you, sir?"

"Huevos Rancheros. And another beer."

The waitress flashed a smile and walked off. Jimmy popped a peanut in his mouth, then reached into a trousers pocket. He pulled out a single key on a chain with a circular tag on it. He tossed it on the table in front of Hal.

"There it is. Address is on the tag."

Hal ran his fingers over the key. "The old guy give you any trouble?"

"Nope. I told him I'd check the place out for him. The fires and all. All the old fucker wants to talk about is that *Red Desert* shoot. Not one of my favorite topics."

"I hear you," Hal sipped from his water glass and plucked a peanut from the bowl. He noticed Jimmy staring at him. "What?"

"Are you okay, man?"

"Yeah. Why?"

Jimmy glanced around at the other patrons and dropped his voice. "Aren't you a little freaked out? About what happened the other night?"

Hal shrugged his shoulders. "I was for a while. Right after it happened."

Jimmy leaned over the table. "What the hell went wrong?" His voice was tense as he spat out the words.

The waitress walked up to their table with two frosted mugs. The men leaned back in their chairs as she placed the beers in front of them. They watched her walk away and Jimmy leaned in again.

"Why was the woman there?"

"I don't know."

"You were supposed to make sure she was working."

"Keep your voice down," Hal said. He leaned over the table and whispered. "Listen to me, Jimmy. She works at that damn boutique every Thursday night. I watched her for weeks. I don't know why the hell she was at Ford's house. As I told you over the phone last night, everything's cool. I didn't leave any traces."

Jimmy was silent, staring off to his right. After a moment, he sipped more beer and again leaned over the table.

"Well, you may think everything's cool, but I'm spooked."

Hal looked at him, eyes bugged out. "Boo!"

Jimmy shook his head. "You are such an asshole." He lifted his beer mug and drank, then looked around. "But you got the Oscar?"

"Yeah."

"And left the letter?"

Hal nodded, reached over and zipped open a pocket on his backpack. "Found this too. With all the crap on his shelves he might not even know I took it." He handed Jimmy a photo.

"Is this the daughter?"

"Gotta be. "Ford's only other kid is a son with another ex-wife."

"Who's the guy with the beard?"

"I don't know." Jimmy handed the photo across the table. Hal looked at it for a moment and replaced it in the backpack. He took a hit off his beer mug and looked around at the celebrity photos on the walls.

"Quite a gallery. All these people actually been in here?"

"Probably. I read somewhere that one night Lee Marvin rode his motorcycle through the front door and right up to the bar."

"Get outta here."

"No lie." Jimmy held up a peanut. "Not only that. Alan Shepard took one of these to the moon and back."

"Bullshit."

"That's what I heard."

Hal laughed and flipped a shell across the table. He drank from his mug and looked around the restaurant. "Think Ford's been in here?"

"Wouldn't surprise me."

The waitress approached the table with their orders. She set them down and asked, "Anything else I can get you fellas?"

The two men shook their heads as they looked up at her. Hal picked a peanut out of the bowl and held it up. "My friend here says one of these things went to the moon with Alan Shepard. True?"

"So the story goes."

The waitress flashed Hal a big wink as she walked off. He turned to Jimmy, who shrugged and said, "See? What'd I tell you?"

The two men ate in silence, looking around the restaurant. At one point, Hal drew Jimmy's attention to a TV star being shown to a table in the rear. A young woman wearing a short floral-patterned skirt appeared to be glued to the star's right flank.

After they finished their meal the waitress approached the table with the check. She picked up the empty plates and looked at Jimmy.

"I've seen you in here before, Hon, but first time for your friend here?"

"Yeah. He lives in the Valley. Doesn't get out here that much."

"Oh, you poor dear," she said as she patted Hal on the back. "Y'awl don't be a stranger, now, you hear?"

"Anyplace that sends peanuts to the moon is fine with me," Hal said. She laughed and he handed her several bills and told her to keep the change.

"Thanks, fellas."

The two men exited the restaurant and Jimmy immediately lit up a cigarette. "So, I'll see you tomorrow?"

"Right," Hal said. "We'll take my van up there. Load it up with the stuff we'll need." He ushered Jimmy away from two couples checking out the menu in the front window. "And listen, Jimmy, don't twist your drawers into a knot. Things are gonna be just fine. Ford is going to be dealing with the cops. He won't see us coming."

"You don't think we should lay low for a while?"

"No. We stick to the plan."

Jimmy took a deep puff off his cigarette and shook his head. "All right, but it still makes me a little skittish."

"Relax. We'll be fine."

They shook hands and parted. Hal watched Jimmy walk south, then caught the light and strolled north toward the Santa Monica Pier. The breeze had picked up, sending the smell of the ocean into his nostrils.

It unnerved him that Jimmy felt the way he did. The accident with Ford's girlfriend bugged the shit out him too, but it couldn't be helped. He felt secure that he hadn't left any traces behind him. He didn't see how it was possible he could be connected to the drowning.

Ahead on the pier rose the Ferris wheel, sparkling in the sunshine. Memories began to wash over him. His daughter always liked going on that ride. She squealed with delight. Then they'd have some cotton candy and watch the old Asian men leaning over the railing, waiting for their rods and cane poles to bend with a bite. One time a fish landed in front of her. She looked at it in awe as it flopped around on the boardwalk. She'd wanted Daddy to tell her the fish was going to be okay. He said it would. She believed him.

Hal stood by a traffic light, looking out at the pier, wondering if she'd still believe him. Thanks to Ford, he'd never know. At that moment someone bumped into him from behind. He turned to see a homeless man wearing an orange stocking cap on his head punching the walk button on the pole. The man shifted his weight from one foot to the other, mumbling to himself as he repeatedly hit the button.

Hal shoved the guy. "Hey, man, why don't you watch where you're going?"

Stocking Cap hit the button one more time and turned to him. "What? Now? You talkin' to me?"

"Yeah, man, I'm talkin' to you. You almost knocked me over. Watch where the fuck you're goin'."

"Yup, yup, okay, will do. Gotta go now. Getting' tired.

Gotta move. He already saw me."

He turned around and stared at a man sitting on a bench a few yards away. Hal followed his gaze. The man on the bench was watching Stocking Cap. He wore a porkpie hat, just like the guy in the picture Hal had taken from Ford's house.

Stocking Cap shuffled across the street as Porkpie rose from the bench and continued to watch him. Hal strolled toward the bench. As he walked by, he stared at Porkpie. He couldn't tell if it was the same person in the picture. That one had a full beard. It couldn't be the same guy. Hal passed by him and turned around. Porkpie walked to the corner and looked in the direction of Stocking Cap.

Lots of men wore those kinds of hats. Hal was imagining things. Paranoia. That's all it was.

Chapter Nine

"You've got to watch where the little arrow is going. The cursor."

"I am, but it keeps skittering away from me."

I was sitting at Mavis's desk. She was on the speakerphone. After she'd convinced me to get the cell phone she'd begun to coach me in the use of her computer. I was a slow learner. However, she'd written down the instructions as to how to boot it up and connect to the Internet. So here I sat, actually on the World Wide Web for crissakes, looking for Jack Boylston's list of credits. I kept following her instructions, silently cursing the cursor. Now I know why they call it that.

She laughed and said, "The Internet Movie Database is at the corner of the desk top."

"There's a potted plant and a picture of your husband at the corner of your desk."

"Eddie, the desktop is the computer screen."

"Oh."

"Up in the right hand corner you'll see an icon with 'imdb' under it. Click on that."

I did as ordered and up popped the site. "Got it."

"At the top of the page you'll see 'search.' Click on the highlighted arrows. A menu drops down. Click on 'names,' type in Jack Boylston in the next box and click on 'Go.'"

I clicked and pecked and a list of names appeared.

"Bingo," I said.

"Jack Boylston's name should be at the top. Click on it and his list of credits will come up."

Amazingly it did. Then the door opened and my search ended. Coming through the opening was Mike Ford.

"Okay, kiddo," I said into the phone. "I think I'm on the right track. Thanks for the help."

I hung up and took Mike's outstretched hand. His face started to crumble and I wrapped my arms around him.

"Sorry for your loss, man."

"Good to see you, Eddie."

"Same here. I was going to call you this afternoon. How you doing?"

"Hanging in there. Been a tough couple of days."

"Yeah." He yanked a couple of tissues from the box on the desk and blew his nose.

"The two of you were good together."

"Thanks. I thought we were too."

He sat down in front of Mavis's desk. His face looked drawn, but despite that, he still had all the trappings of a leading man. Broad shoulders, jet-black hair, chiseled features. Mike was about my height, a shade over six feet. He wore khakis and a blue blazer over a white polo shirt.

"So what's the LAPD saying?"

"They were calling it an accident until I told them about the missing Oscar."

"And now they're figuring homicide?"

"Possibly. Janice hit her head on the edge of the pool. She could have just slipped. There was a pretty good dent in a bottle of wine. Right now they don't have anything to tie the robbery and the drowning together." He shrugged his shoulders. "So I don't know what the hell's going on." He looked at me and pulled an envelope from the inside pocket of his blazer.

"You got a beer back there in that den of yours?"

"That I do."

I went into my apartment and grabbed two cans of Bud along with a couple of glasses. When I got back to Mavis's desk, Mike was looking at the computer screen.

"IMDB? What were you trying to find?"

"As a matter of fact, a film you did. With 'red' in the title?"

"Yeah, *Red Desert*. Out in the Mojave. Remake of an old 1949 potboiler. Some say I improved on it. I think the jury's still out."

"You remember a guy in it by the name of Jack Boylston?"

"Boylston." He thought for a moment as I jotted the title on a Post-It. "Yeah, right. Wiry little guy. He played a stagecoach driver."

I scrolled down the list of Jack's credits until I came across *Red Desert* and clicked on it. "There you are. Directed by Mike Ford." I looked down the cast list. "Whoa, also playing the role of the Pecos Kid."

"Well, I didn't want to take on the damn part, but the money guys said I should for box office. Turned out to be kind of a pain in the butt."

"How so?"

"Tough shoot. Heat, script problems, casting snafus, you name it."

I fumbled with a couple of keys and finally managed to close the site and shut down the computer. I opened the two beers, filled the glasses and handed him one.

"To better times," I said. He raised his glass and we both drank.

"Are you working on something now?" he said.

"Doing a sitcom over at Disney. Why?"

"No, I meant as a shamus." He picked up the envelope in front of him and pulled out some folded sheets of paper. "I don't know if someone's playing a sick joke or what, but take at look at these." He unfolded the sheets, separated two and handed them to me. "This one with the stamp I got a week ago. The cops have the originals."

A duplicate of an envelope bore a Van Nuys postmark and what appeared to be a computer generated mailing label. Scrawled across the second sheet of paper in letters cut out from various publications were the words "Before The Beginning There Was Me."

"This is weird," I said as I ran my fingers over the letters. Some were newsprint, others glossy, as if from magazines.

"What's weird?"

"That sitcom over at Disney? The name of it is *Before the Beginning*."

"You're kidding?"

I shook my head.

He handed me the other two pages. "This one was left where my Oscar was sitting."

One of the sheets was a duplicate of another envelope with cut-out letters spelling "Mike Ford" pasted on it.

Glued on the second sheet of paper were more letters revealing the words "This Is But The Beginning."

I looked up at him. "What do you think 'This' refers to?"

"Could be the missing Oscar or Janice's death. I'm not sure which. Maybe she barged in on someone."

"Or someone slammed her head into the pool and then took the Oscar." I sipped from my glass. "Any idea who'd be behind something like this?"

He shook his head. "Not a clue."

I held both messages and looked from one to the other. "They're practically identical. Except for the wording."

"Looks like the same person made both of them."

"Anybody in your past who's carrying a grudge?"

He thought for a moment. "Hell, Eddie, I don't know. You run into a lot of people in this town. Egos all over the goddamn place. Sometimes it doesn't take much to put somebody's nose out of joint."

"This might not qualify as a grudge, but the guy Boylston I mentioned?"

"Yeah, what about him?"

"His wife hired me a few weeks back. Seems like Jack sort of disappeared. He didn't go far. I found him after a couple of days. But his wife called me yesterday saying he'd taken off again. By the time I talked to them this morning he'd come back." I sipped from my beer. "The thing is, during our conversation he said an odd thing."

"What?"

"According to Jack you treated him like dirt during the shoot. His words, not mine."

Mike swallowed some beer and said, "How so?"

"He didn't elaborate. Matter of fact, Jack tends to forget things, so I don't know what to believe."

"Can't imagine why he would say that."

I poured more beer into my glass and looked at the pages in front of me. "You've got your own production company, right?"

"Parkwood Films. Over at Paramount."

"Fired anybody lately?"

Again he thought and shook his head. "Not that I can think of. I've got a partner that's more hands-on, day-to-day than I am. But he runs everything by me." He poured the last of the beer into his glass and drained it.

"Listen, Eddie, I came by here wanting to hire you. To see if you can find out who the hell sent these things."

"You don't want the police to deal with them?"

"Well, as I said, they've got the originals. Unless there's a connection between the second one and what happened the other night, I don't know what the hell the cops can do. A crank letter could be totally unrelated."

"Except for the fact that it looks like the same person constructed both of them."

"Right." He sighed and leaned back in his chair. "What do you say? That sitcom got you tied up every day?"

"I'm booked for another week. But I don't imagine I'll be called all the time. I can do some poking around."

"Your fee gonna bust me?"

I caught the grin on his face. "I'll work within your budget."

"You want me to sign a contract?"

"I'll have Mavis draw something up." He nodded and

got to his feet. "What about your exes? They have any issues with you?"

"My first moved back east. I rarely talk to her. Brent's mother remarried. Courtney's mother and I get along all right. If they've got a problem with me, I haven't heard about it."

"You figuring on telling Courtney's mother about this?"

"I don't think so. At least for now." He took a pair of sunglasses from the breast pocket of his blazer.

I held up the four pages. "Can I keep these?"

"I copied them for you," he said as he handed me the envelope they came in. He stuck out his hand. "Anything you need from me, you've got my numbers." He walked to the front door.

"I'll see what I can do. Who did you talk to at LAPD?"

"A Lieutenant Rivers. I think that was his name."

"Charlie Rivers. I know him." He nodded and opened the door. "Sorry about Janice, Mike. I was glad I got to know her."

"I'm glad you did too." He gave me a little salute, put on his dark glasses and went out the door.

I finished my beer and looked at the sheets of paper in front of me. Somebody using scissors and glue, pasting letters together like the idle play task of a child. But the messages didn't come across to me as being child's play. Someone had a point to make. Who? Jack Boylston? Was he faking it when he said he couldn't remember where he'd been? Was somebody prodding him? I ran my fingers over both sets of letters. "Before The Beginning There Was Me." "This Is But The Beginning." Beginning of what? A fragment from the past looming in front of Mike Ford, trying to get his attention?

***

I called around to a couple of video stores and found a copy of *Red Desert*. After I bought it, I stopped for a burger and got back to the office to see a message from Mavis, reminding me to phone Mike Ford. I called her back and gave her the rundown of our meeting. She told me to let her know if I needed any more help with the computer.

I poured myself a drink and settled in with the movie. The plot was pretty typical melodrama. Mike was the Pecos Kid, hired by Ulysses S. Grant to discover who's stealing gold bullion. Jack Boylston had a nifty little part as the stagecoach driver and acquitted himself admirably. I sometimes was able to detect behind Mike's eyes a look of panic, as if he was wondering why the hell he was sweating his ass off in the middle of the desert.

In the scenes they had together, I didn't see any evidence of Mike treating Jack like dirt. The two characters they played were allies within the plot. But then, what went on behind the camera was another story.

Near the end of the saga I sat up on the edge of my chair. A young boy showed up to take care of the bad guy's horse. He looked familiar. I reversed the DVD and froze it on the kid's face filling the frame. I watched the end credits twice but couldn't detect the character's name listed.

When I was surfing the Internet Movie Database earlier, I noticed that the cast list also included those who were uncredited. I stopped the movie and booted up Mavis's computer again. Clicking on the IMDB icon got me to the site. I scrolled down the cast list and saw "see more." After clicking on it up came "rest of cast listed alphabetically."

There weren't many names on this list, but the one playing "stable boy" was a Michael Patterson. I clicked on his name and was directed to a page where Michael Patterson, aka Mickey Patterson's latest credit was a TV show called *Before the Beginning*.

More reel life collided with reality. Thinking he would need to know, I called Mike on his cell and filled him in. After a moment he said, "Why don't you come over here in the morning, Eddie. The fact that you know two guys who worked with me on a dumb-ass movie years ago is a little weird. Maybe we better get on my computer and see if there's any more oddities. Come on over about eleven and I'll rustle us up some brunch."

"You got it," I said. I broke the connection and looked at the computer screen. I'm not a big gambler, but the odds of me knowing three people involved in the same movie seemed a long shot. More importantly, how were the three tied together? Did the connection have something to do with the disappearance of a gold statuette and a possible murder?

Chapter Ten

Hal had never driven up into Kagel Canyon. Now he knew why. Not a green lawn to be seen anywhere, and rocks, nothing but rocks. Every house looked like a ramshackle shed waiting to be blown over with the next gust of wind. The neighborhood resembled many of those found in and around Barstow, where that damn movie was shot. *Red Desert.* The one Mike Ford had stolen from him.

Even thinking of it now provoked a knot in his stomach. He reached between his legs for the bottle of water and put it to his lips. It was warm. He rinsed his mouth and spit out the window of the van. The temperature must be in the nineties and it was only a little after nine.

He looked to his right and saw Jimmy staring out the passenger window, his mouth agape. "Are you watching the map?" He'd printed them out from Google.

Jimmy picked up a page from the pile on his lap and leaned forward to look through the windshield. "Yeah, we're almost there. Keep an eye out for an adobe-looking house and turn left. You need to get a GPS, Hal."

"Yeah, right. And a new air conditioner. Not to mention a new van. Maybe I should get an SUV, with OnStar and a driver while I'm at it." He shook his head. "Gimme a break."

Jimmy gestured off to the east. "Those fires look awful

close. You sure we're gonna be safe up here?"

"We'll be okay."

All morning long his friend had been grousing about the wisdom of what they were planning. Hal was sick of it. He looked off to his right at the ridges dotted with brush and trees. He had to admit, though, that if the fires continued they could become an issue. "Are you sure Boylston isn't going to come up here?"

"He told me his wife won't let him drive."

"Well, what about her?"

"It's too cool down in Venice. No reason for them to come up here." Jimmy picked up the printout again and pointed ahead of them. "There. That looks like it. Slow down."

Hal slowed the van as they approached a maroon stucco house resembling a dwelling one might see in the Mexican desert. A wooden fence surrounded it on three sides. A sliding metal gate fronted a concrete driveway. Hal turned left and slowly drove up a narrow paved lane. On the right sat a cylindrical tank that looked like the water supply for the neighborhood.

Off to his left an elderly woman hung laundry on a clothesline next to a small house with a sagging front porch. She had a large floppy hat on her head and wore baggy shorts and a white blouse. The woman stopped what she was doing and stared at them as they passed.

"Think she's going to bother us?" Jimmy said.

"I knew an actor who used to live in this canyon," Hal said. "He told me nobody paid any attention to anybody else. That was the main reason he moved up here."

"She looks kind of nosy to me."

Hal slapped the steering wheel with his fists and shook his head. "You've got to stop being so goddamn paranoid, Jimmy. You're driving me nuts."

"Okay, okay. Just saying."

Hal turned into the next driveway and stopped near the front door of a small house. Two lone trees in the front yard provided little shade. No grass, just more red dirt and scattered rocks outlining the driveway. The house was painted white with red trim around the windows, faded from the sun. A small redwood patio jutted from the east side of the structure next to the front door. There was a round table with an umbrella protruding from the center of it. A barbecue grill sat in one corner. A single-car garage occupied the end of the driveway. On the roof of the house was perched a TV satellite dish.

"This is it," Hal said. "I'll open up. Grab one of those boxes in the back."

Hal crawled from the van and climbed the two steps to the front door as Jimmy opened the rear of the van. He pulled open a battered wooden screen door, turned the key in the lock and pushed. Hot dead air greeted him. The living room lay in front of him, a kitchen off to the right. Ahead of him stretched a hallway with a bathroom at the end of it. A sofa sat against the far wall of the living room, flanked by two recliners. In the corner sat an old television set. A small table occupied the kitchen, next to the door leading out to the patio.

Behind him, Jimmy nudged his way through the door,

a cardboard box in his arms. "Damn, no air conditioning."

Hal gestured to a north-facing window in the kitchen. "A unit there. We're not going to be here long enough. We better just open the windows."

He walked toward the bathroom at the end of the hall. Doors to two bedrooms were open on either side of the corridor. He entered the larger of the two and called back to Jimmy. "Bring the box in here." The bedroom had two windows, one of them plugged with another air conditioning unit.

Jimmy came in behind him and set the cardboard box on the double bed. The two men spent the next few moments opening windows. The smaller bedroom also had an a/c unit. Gradually a cross breeze from outside started filtering through the house, removing some of the stuffiness. They each carried in another box from the van and put them on the double bed. The cartons contained a variety of toys and games.

Hal picked up a stuffed giraffe and turned it over in his hands. "All these things were my daughter's. Think they'll work, Jimmy? They've been in storage for a while. Maybe they're outdated."

"They'll be fine. My sister's kid's about her age. She's got a lot of the same stuff. That Wii you bought was a good touch." Hal nodded and joined Jimmy in unloading the boxes.

The two men froze as they heard someone knocking on the front door. A woman's voice called out, "Hello?" The two men looked at each other.

"I told you she was going to be nosy," Jimmy hissed,

his voice full of panic.

"All right, listen," Hal whispered. "Follow my lead. I'm Boylston's nephew. Do some ad libbing." Jimmy nodded and they stepped into the hallway and walked toward the front door.

Shading her eyes from the sun as she peered through the screen door was the woman they'd seen hanging up laundry.

"Hello there," Hal said. "Can we help you?"

"Well, my name is Clara Jesperson. I saw you drive up. I haven't seen you here before. Just thought I would introduce myself. Are you friends of Helen and Jack?"

"Actually, I'm Jack's nephew," Hal said. "My name is Howard." He gestured to Jimmy. "This is my friend Walt."

Jimmy raised his hand in greeting. "Hi there, Mrs. Jesperson."

"We're screenwriting partners," Hal continued. "We have an office down in LA, but there's construction going on next door. Makes it harder than heck to concentrate. Uncle Jack was kind enough to let us use his place up here to write."

"Oh, I see. Well, isn't that nice of him?"

"Sure is," Hal said. "We're just dropping some stuff off and airing out the place."

She pulled a red bandana from her pocket and wiped the back of her neck. "He never told me he had a nephew."

"Really? Well, I just moved down here from Seattle not too long ago. I haven't seen him for a number of years. Maybe he just forgot."

"Oh my, yes, he does tend to do that." Clara put the

bandana in her pocket and stepped away from the door. "Okay, then. Didn't mean to pry. Just was curious, you know. A vehicle one doesn't recognize. You never can tell these days."

"You sure can't," Jimmy said. "Hope we didn't alarm you."

"Oh, goodness no. I just kinda like to look after the house for Helen. They don't get up here that often."

"No, I suppose not," Hal said. "Much cooler for them down in Venice."

"My yes," Clara said as she descended the steps. "I'll let you go. You boys are busy."

"Pleasure meeting you, Clara. You take care now." Hal watched her as she tottered back toward her house. He closed the front door and turned to Jimmy. "Good going, Walt." The two men laughed and high-fived each other. "Let's get those boxes unloaded and clean out the van."

While Hal placed the toys and games against the wall in the corner of the bedroom, Jimmy brought a cooler into the house and transferred the contents to the small refrigerator. Juices, yogurt and snacks.

They left the windows cracked open, Hal locked the front door and they started driving back down the hill. Clara Jesperson was hanging another load of wash on the clothesline. Hal and Jimmy waved to her as they drove by. She raised her arm in greeting.

"Do you think she's got a key?" Jimmy asked.

"It wouldn't surprise me," Hal said. "Let's hope she doesn't decide to use it."

"Or to call Boylston's wife."

Hal looked over at Jimmy and nodded. "Yeah, right." The van turned the corner and started back down the canyon.

***

Clara Jesperson watched the beat-up van drive away. She couldn't recall if Helen Boylston had ever told her about any family she and Jack had. Of course, with Jack starting to lose his memory one wondered what he did or did not remember any more. Such a burden for Helen. Clara wondered if she should give her a call and tell her about the two young men. Well, I suppose it's none of my business.

She finished pinning the sheets to the line and ran her hand over the first load she'd hung. For goodness sake, dry already. Going to be another day to stay indoors.

Chapter Eleven

Nottingham Avenue snaked through the hills below Griffith Park Observatory. The narrow street had parking restricted to one side. Mike Ford's house was white, two storied, with red adobe tiles on the roof, a safeguard against fires fanned by the Santa Anas. Four palm trees filled the miniscule front yard, their fronds sighing in the warm Sunday morning breeze. A covered walkway led from the left side of the house to a double garage. A small driveway lay next to a wooden gate on the right side of the structure. Yellow police tape stretched across the entry.

I nudged my car into the parking space, walked to the front door, and rang the bell. Iron bars covered the windows, almost a necessity in greater Los Angeles. Above the entrance a small wrought-iron balcony protruded from French doors. It was supported by two white columns. I looked across the street. Nothing but woods. Tree roots were exposed from winter rains, which always followed the fires. A never-ending cycle. Mike had a nice place up here. Secluded. But apparently not enough to keep a burglar off the premises.

I'd been up here on a few occasions. The last time we'd watched a movie together, a rough-cut of one of his latest ventures. He had graciously welcomed my comments. I doubted whether they had anything to do with the movie's huge opening weekend grosses, but it was nice to be asked.

Mike opened the door and stepped out.

"Morning. Damn, it's already hot. You staying cool in that place of yours?"

"I yearn for a Midwestern blizzard," I said. We turned to look downhill as a battered brown van backfired on its way up the incline. "You have any danger of fires up here?"

"Yeah, we have to be careful." He gestured to the van. "Backfiring heaps like that don't help."

I pointed to the police tape. "So the guy came through that gate?"

"Over it," Mike said. "It's always locked."

"Your alarm was off?"

"Janice disarmed it when she got here."

"The neighbors hear anything?"

Mike took a couple of steps toward the curb and pointed downhill as the van lumbered up the street. The driver's face was obscured by a big floppy straw hat. "A young guy and a gal live in that house. I only know them to wave hello." He pointed in the opposite direction. "Fred and Susan Morgan over there. Both lawyers. I talked to everyone. They didn't hear a thing."

We walked back to the front door and he ushered me inside. The house was cool. Large comfortable chairs and sofas filled a living room on the right. To the other side of the entry was a dining room, seating for eight.

"Too early for a Bloody Mary?"

"Not for me," I replied.

Mike guided me down a central hallway underneath a

curved staircase leading to the second story. His kitchen was to the left, a door connected it to the dining room. A huge butcher block sat in the middle. A breakfast bar divided the room. In front of the rear windows sat a table and four chairs.

Across the hallway an arch opened onto a den. Mike led me into the room and walked to one of two shelves filled with books, pictures and knickknacks.

"The Oscar was sitting here," he said.

I saw a Golden Globe and an Emmy occupying the space he indicated. Behind me a huge stone fireplace filled the center of the room. The other two walls had sliding glass doors in them. One set opened to the pool. I walked through them onto the concrete deck. More yellow tape stretched from the corners to the diving board. A glass-topped table with an umbrella in the middle sat to my left.

Mike came up behind me. "She apparently slipped and hit her head there." He pointed to a spot four feet from the diving board. "The deck was wet. I don't know how much wine she had to drink. She might have been a little tipsy."

A narrow strip of lawn ran along the length of the pool. A gas grill sat under the kitchen windows. The entire backyard was surrounded by a wire fence, tall hedges and more palm trees.

"What do you think, Mike, an accident?"

He sat down at the table. I pulled out a chair and looked at him as he stared into the pool.

"I don't know, Eddie. Seems too coincidental that the

Oscar would disappear the same night. I think she discovered somebody taking it and he hit her on the head with it."

"The cops find any other evidence of blunt force trauma?"

"That's the weird thing. All they've told me is that she hit her head on the lip of the pool. Doesn't make sense to me. If someone broke in, why would they want just the Oscar? Hell, she'd have given it to them. The Academy will only replace it. They can't sell the damn thing without drawing suspicion to themselves."

"The police find any prints?"

"Apparently not. Whoever broke in covered their tracks pretty well." He ran one hand over his head and sat up on the edge of his chair. "Her cell phone was here on the table. There was a message on it from me. I'd called her when I was fifteen minutes away. I could have passed the son of a bitch coming up the hill."

He pinched the bridge of his nose and took a couple of deep breaths, fighting back tears. "Ah, shit. She had so much to look forward to. Getting her MFA in the spring. Now, it's--" He stopped, his lips clenched. I reached over and gripped his shoulder.

"Sorry," he said as he stood up. "Let's see about those Bloody Marys."

We walked back into the kitchen and I sat at the breakfast bar as Mike mixed the drinks. We tapped glasses and he set about pulling omelet ingredients from the refrigerator.

"So what did you think of *Red Desert*?"

"I enjoyed it. Good to see a western for a change."

"Well, considering all the problems we had on the damn thing, I guess it turned out all right. Made a little money.

"I do remember that Patterson kid from the shoot. He was very inquisitive. Watched every scene being shot. No wonder he's still in the business."

"Have you seen him since the movie?"

He shook his head. "Hadn't thought of him until you mentioned his name."

"Would he have reason to carry a grudge against you?"

"Not that I can think of. Hell, he barely would've been in his teens."

"I'll talk to him tomorrow," I said. The pleasant aroma of eggs and ham filled the kitchen. I sipped on my Bloody Mary and jotted down a couple of notes.

"I'm still trying to wrap my head around what Jack Boylston said about you."

"How do you suppose he formed that opinion?"

"I'm not sure. He's beginning to show some signs of dementia and a lot of bitterness." Mike dished up two omelets, set them on the bar, along with toast and jam, and then sat on a stool across from me. "Can you think of any reason he would say something like that?"

Mike forked some omelet into his mouth and thought for a moment. "Man, that was what? Five years back? We spent three months out in Barstow in the fall. Still hotter than hell. I remember on a couple of occasions Jack having some trouble getting his lines right. But hell, that happens to everyone."

"You never had a run-in with him as the director?"

He shook his head as he bit into a piece of toast. "I don't think this was a run-in, but there was one day when he couldn't hit the mark with the horses. It was enough of a medium shot where a stunt driver couldn't be used. I think we went through a dozen takes or so. I finally decided we could cut away and pick him up in a closer shot."

"Jack have a problem with that?"

"No, it worked fine. I don't know if you remember the sequence, but there were two grizzled old farts sitting in front of the saloon?"

I thought back and recalled the moment. "Right. They had their chairs leaning up against the wall."

"Exactly. I had them see the stage coming and push away from the saloon. It was a pretty seamless cut."

I sipped from my Bloody Mary and dug into my food. The situation always arises with actors where they're asked if they can ride a horse, a motorcycle, dance the tango, or some other specific task. The natural tendency is to say hell yes, you name it, I can do it. The lure of having one's face up on the big screen can sometimes make an actor think he has superpowers. I wondered if Jack maybe felt like he had ruined a scene.

"Did Boylston exhibit any resentment that he couldn't get the shot you wanted?"

"No, I don't think so. Not that I heard of anyway. I thought he did damn well under the circumstances. I mean, Christ, four horses?"

We polished off our plates and I drank the rest of my

Bloody Mary as I watched Mike load the dishwasher. He poured us coffee and we walked upstairs. Mike had printed out pages of cast and crew lists for the movies he'd worked on. The pile was considerable.

"I don't know what good these will do, but I made some notes about several people on those lists. Just some things I remember about them. Maybe it'll give you something to go on." He leaned back in his desk chair as I glanced through the pages. "You remember when your ex-wife was murdered, Eddie?"

"All the time." After that episode happened a few months back, Mike had talked me through some of it. Our conversations had been invaluable.

"And the rage you felt?"

"It was intense," I said.

"Exactly. When I came home the other night and found Janice, it consumed me. Burned. I felt like I'd been violated. Almost like a piece of me had been ripped out. Never felt that way before." He leaned forward and swallowed some coffee. "Aw, Christ, Eddie, I hope this isn't just some dumb-ass prank that went wrong."

"Hell of a lot of trouble for just a prank." I shuffled the pages together and slid them into a manila envelope. "Did you find anything else missing? Maybe the Oscar was just to throw you off."

"I never thought of that." He rose from behind the desk, picked up his coffee cup and headed for the door. "Let's take a look in the den."

We went downstairs and approached the shelf where the Oscar had sat.

"I've got this housekeeper who likes to dust. And move stuff around. I keep telling her to leave things in place, but she doesn't listen." He started looking over the contents of the shelves.

"How long has she worked for you?"

"Years."

"And she's got access to the house I suppose?"

"Yeah, but I'm pretty sure she—" He stopped and stared at a spot on a shelf. "Wait a minute."

"What?"

"You remember that day the two of us took Courtney to Disneyland?"

"Sure do. She didn't know who I was at first because of that damn beard I had."

"I gave that young couple from Arizona an autograph in exchange for taking a picture of the three of us."

"Right."

He turned to face me. "The photo's missing, Eddie. Someone's got a picture of my daughter."

Chapter Twelve

As Hal came over the Cahuenga Pass he wasn't sure why he wanted to drive past Ford's house. It was nowhere near where he lived in Van Nuys.

After he and Jimmy had left the toys in the Kagel Canyon house and talked to the old lady next door, they'd checked out the neighborhood a bit, then driven back to Hal's place. Jimmy left for Venice and Hal sat in his sweltering apartment, smoking a small bowl. After a few minutes, restlessness enveloped him like a wet wool blanket. He plopped a floppy hat on his head and left.

Now, as his old van lumbered up Nottingham, Hal realized that he was acting just like when he was a kid and had trapped a mouse. He knew the little creature would still be in the box when he got home from school. Yet he had to scurry down to the basement to see for himself. To make sure.

Ford's house was similar. Hal needed to see if there was a police presence in the wake of the woman drowning in the pool. If someone was watching the mouse. Had the big movie star hired security? Was there a guard on duty?

He rounded a bend and spied the house. A car was parked in the driveway. It didn't look like a cop car, even though there was yellow police tape stretched across the gate he'd jumped over. Ford and another man stood in front of the house. Wait a minute. The visitor had a porkpie hat on his head. Another goddamn porkpie. Like the one he'd seen in Santa Monica yesterday. Was it the same guy? Hal couldn't tell.

He shifted into a lower gear and the van suddenly backfired. Shit! The two men turned to look at him. Hal kept moving. The big hat would shield his face. If Ford had brought in security, that could complicate things. But porkpie's car was unmarked. Still unnerving, though. He'd have to be careful when he dropped off the next letter.

Hal chugged past Ford and the porkpie guy. They glanced at him but then turned away. The van passed behind the visitor's car. He looked sideways and fixed the license plate in his head. He couldn't turn around and drive past the house again to verify the number. Too suspicious. He'd have to wind his way back down Glendower and Catalina to Franklin.

Nottingham made a hairpin turn. When he was out of sight of Ford's house, Hal pulled over and stopped. He picked up his PDA from the seat next to him and tapped in the license number from porkpie's car. The presence of the strange guy was unsettling. The photo he'd taken from Ford's house the other night showed a man wearing the same kind of hat. And now a similar guy stood in front of the house talking to Ford. Hal would bet money it was the person in the picture. So maybe Ford had indeed hired security or a bodyguard. That was good. The letters obviously had made an impression on him. Let the mouse sweat inside the box.

Chapter Thirteen

The look of helplessness on Mike's face when he realized
the photo was missing kept me company as I headed west
on the Santa Monica Freeway. We'd searched the place,
hoping that maybe the housekeeper had moved it. No
luck. It was indeed missing. He debated whether or not to
inform Courtney's mother, finally concluding that she
needed to be told. I asked him if he was going to notify
the police. He said no. They'd been informed of the initial
break-in. The place had been dusted, but hadn't turned
up any prints. Mike didn't think LAPD would put much
priority on a missing photograph. I tended to agree with
him. That didn't take away from the fact that we were
both concerned. Grilling Mickey Patterson tomorrow was
of prime importance.

But first, I had this itch I had to scratch.

***

It didn't take me long to find him. He was walking down
Ocean Avenue, sizing up the panhandling prospects. A
young couple pushing a stroller ignored him. He flipped
them the bird as they went by, then stopped to paw
through a trash bin as I walked up to him.

"Hey, remember me?"

His head snapped up and he wiped his hands on his
shirt. After a moment he pointed at me.

"I do indeed, sir. I recognize the hat. How are you

doing this fine day?"

"Good. How was the Big Mac?"

"I opted for a Whopper. Char-broiled. Much healthier."

How that assessment played out against the fact that he had just finished pawing through a trash bin was beyond me.

"And it was outstanding. As were the fries. My thanks to you, sir."

I pulled my money clip out and separated a double sawbuck from the other bills.

"This is yours if you give me some information."

He eyed the twenty, almost salivating. "What kind of information?"

"There was a guy here yesterday, just after you left. Orange stocking cap on his head? Beard, denim shirt? Ring a bell?"

The guy stared at the twenty bucks, watching me smooth out the creases. "Yes, sir, I know the gentleman."

"What's his name?"

"Tired Reggie."

"Tired Reggie? Why do you call him that?"

"He always says he's tired."

"What's his last name?"

"One of life's mysteries, my friend. I know him only by Tired Reggie. Everybody calls him that."

"Have you seen him today?"

"Earlier. Out on the pier."

"How long ago?"

"About an hour."

I handed him the twenty-dollar bill and he stuffed it in

his pocket as if it was going to disintegrate in the sunshine.

"Thank you, kind sir," he said. I started to walk away. "Considerably hot out here. Might need to partake of a beer. That okay, mister?"

"Knock yourself out. Far be it for me to deprive some unfortunate soul of a little relief from the heat. I headed for the Santa Monica Pier, on the lookout for an orange stocking cap.

Reggie. The name tumbled around in my head. The only one that came to me was Reggie Benson, a young guy that was a military policeman with me in the Army. We served together in Korea, a few years after that futile turmoil in Vietnam. He was several years younger than me. In fact, I think he was only seventeen and had to have his parents sign for him so he could enlist. His age didn't impede his effectiveness as a military cop, though. He was fearless, tough, and wore the uniform with pride.

A steady stream of traffic poured into the parking lot north of the pier. Dads toting coolers and folding chairs slogged through the sand. Umbrellas popped up. Families staked out real estate, fleeing the stifling heat of the San Fernando Valley and the inland basin. There was no sign of an orange stocking cap.

As I continued toward the end of the pier I began to recall that sweltering Saturday night. Reggie and I were walking a beat in one of the Korean villages outside a military post. The stench of kimchi floated from tiny restaurants along the street. The smell hung in the night air, inescapable. It was the weekend after payday, a time for GIs to cut loose and throw their money away on booze and hookers. We were charged with persuading them to do otherwise. We weren't always successful.

There was always a troublemaker. This one came stumbling out of one of the door-to-door whore-houses. He was hopped up on a combination of booze and drugs, his arm around the neck of a small Korean woman. He was a big muscle-bound staff sergeant and he had a knife in one hand, the blade pressed against the hooker's throat. We told him to lose the knife. He told us to go to hell. She had cheated him out of his money he said. We flanked him and he tossed the woman aside and lunged for me. The swipe of his blade caught me on the right arm and blood started to flow. He backed me up against a wall, defiance and malice in his eyes. I couldn't make my arm work properly to draw my firearm.

Reggie grabbed a shirt off a curbside clothing rack. He wrapped it around his left arm and cracked the sergeant on the head with his baton. The drunk spun around and advanced on him. I don't know where the kid learned his moves, but it wasn't more than a few seconds before the staff sergeant was lying on the sidewalk, unconscious. We called for someone to pick him up. Reggie used the shirt as a tourniquet on me and saw to it that I got to the infirmary. I never forgot the incident. If it hadn't been for Benson, I would have bought the farm.

Tired Reggie. If indeed it was him. After the Army I'd kept in touch with him for a few months but then lost contact. Last I'd heard he was down in San Diego. He told me that he was thinking of becoming a cop. If the guy in the stocking cap was Reggie Benson, he must have had a change of plans.

I threaded my way through the throngs of people on the pier. Up ahead on the right, leaning over the railing looking down at the beach was someone wearing an orange stocking cap. I came up on his right and watched him for a moment as he bounced back and forth on his feet, leaning on his elbows. He wore his field jacket and watched two kids next to him throwing chunks of bread into the air for the gulls.

"Hey, Reggie."

He straightened up, looked behind him and then turned in my direction. He froze when he saw me. I walked up to him, but he didn't retreat.

"Reggie Benson?"

He ducked his head and scrunched the stocking cap down around his ears. "Yeah, yeah, that's me."

"Second Division in Korea? MP company?"

"I was over there, yeah."

I stuck my hand out. "It's Eddie Collins. Remember me?"

He tentatively reached out and grabbed my hand. "Yup, yup. So you found me, huh? I saw you yesterday. Sitting next to my buddy Tony."

Up close his eyes looked sad, somehow distant. He pulled the cap off his forehead and fiddled with his beard.

"Long time no see, Reggie. How you been?"

"Tired sometimes. But feelin' pretty good today. Nice breeze." Behind him one of the kids shrieked with delight as a seagull flew right in front of them.

"I saw you on the TV once. You an actor now, huh?"

"Occasionally." I leaned on the railing next to him. "So what have you been doing? Heard you were down in San Diego trying to be a cop. What happened?"

"Oh, jeez, Eddie, I don't know. Got tired of it. Had a little trouble and they drummed me out. Probably just as well. Went to Arizona for a coupla years. Nothing panned out there either." He took off his field jacket, rolled it up and stuck it under one arm.

"How long have you been out here?"

"Ah, 'bout a year, I guess."

"You living on the streets?"

"Mostly. Sometimes I luck out and get a bed at one of the shelters. I get kinda tired of them, though. People rip you off, you know?"

I looked at my watch. "You had anything to eat today?"

"Guy outside the 7-Eleven gave me a donut this morning."

"Come on, I'll buy you some lunch." He hesitated and looked around him. "Whatever you want. We've got some catching up to do." He nodded and fell in step with me.

We found an outdoor table under an umbrella at Rusty's Surf Ranch. The kid behind the counter gave me attitude when he saw the homeless guy at my elbow. The color of my money changed his perspective. We sat in the shade and I watched Reggie inhale fish tacos and fries. I had a beer. Reggie said he'd just have a Coke. When his lunch was gone, I asked him if he wanted something else. He looked at me sheepishly and I went back and brought him two more tacos with fries.

As the seagulls flitted around us, Reggie filled me in on what had been happening to him over the last several years. He confessed to having had a little problem dealing with the rigors of discipline at the San Diego Police Academy. He'd gone to Phoenix and worked construction for a time, then odd jobs here and there, day laborer, enough to get by. A friend of his had given him a ride to LA with the promise of a job in a lumberyard. There was no job. He took to the streets and had been living from hand to mouth ever since.

I asked him if he was clean and sober. He swore up and down that he was. Couldn't exist on the streets if he drank or did drugs. He said he'd seen too many guys destroy themselves.

He went on to say he'd briefly flirted with pot some years ago, but that he'd gotten tired of that too.

"How come they call you Tired Reggie?"

He grinned and shook his head. "Aw, I don't know. I think that started when I was at the academy. Guess I got a habit of sayin' I'm tired of this or that. Probably why they kicked me out." He shrugged, slurped up some Coke and tossed a French fry to a gull. "So how's that acting business working out, Eddie?"

"Up and down."

"Yup, yup. I imagine. Tough business."

"Actually, I opened up my own detective agency a few years back."

He jerked his head up. "No kiddin'? Like the dude that lived in that trailer? Up in Malibu, way back when? Rockford. Rockford, yeah, that guy?"

I chuckled and took a pull off my beer. "Not exactly. I don't get in as much trouble as he did."

He nodded his head and munched on his fish taco, sort of mumbling to himself, as if he were audibly processing the information he'd just received.

Then an idea struck me. I didn't know if it was stupid or not, but seeing Reggie sitting across from me vividly brought back the memory of that Saturday night in Korea. Here was the kid who saved my life. He was down on his luck. Maybe I had an opportunity to pay him back.

He finished his food, ran a napkin over his beard and deposited his trash in a nearby receptacle. When he came back to the table, he unfurled his jacket and gave it a shake.

"Hey, thanks for the chow, Eddie." He slipped the jacket on, then looked at his feet, almost as though he was embarrassed for having accepted the meal. "Good seein' you."

I stood up, finished my beer and called to him as he turned to go.

"Hey, Reggie. Where's your stuff?"

"My stuff?"

"Yeah, you know, your stuff. Clothes, things like that?"

"Guy who works at the 7-Eleven lets me keep a bag in the back room."

I pitched the empty beer cup into the trash bin. "Come on, let's go get your bag."

"Huh? What're talkin' about?"

"I'll tell you on the way. Come on."

He pulled his stocking cap down around his ears and

shuffled from one foot to the other. "I don't...I mean, I—"

He stopped talking when I put an arm around his shoulders and propelled us along the pier toward Ocean Avenue and my car. An experiment was about to unfold. I hoped it wouldn't blow up in my face.

Chapter Fourteen

The steel felt good in his hands. Smooth, solid. He'd just finished cleaning the Smith and Wesson 1911. His two rotating fans wafted the faint odor of gun oil through the apartment. Hal hadn't touched the firearm in weeks. He kept it in a cherry wood box under his bed. Found it at a garage sale. A little glue and varnish and good as new. The pistol came from a friend. Acid took care of the serial number.

He wrapped the gun in a terrycloth hand towel and replaced the box under his bed. He grabbed a beer from the fridge on his way back from the bedroom, took a good gulp and reached for his pipe. On the TV another Mike Ford film was running. In this one he was playing a cop. Hal thought it was overrated. He'd muted the movie's sound.

The Doors were coming out of his iPod. The player sat in a small stand, speakers on either side. The sound was somewhat tinny, but better than investing in huge woofers and tweeters. He took a hit off the pipe, held it and leaned back in the sofa. After a moment, he exhaled and watched the smoke dissipate in the swath of the fan.

It had been an interesting day. Truth be told, he hadn't been very confident about how Jimmy had extolled the virtues of the house in Kagel Canyon. But it was perfect. Secluded. Exactly the kind of trap they needed. The old lady, Clara Jesperson, however, had been unexpected. On the surface, she had all the qualities of being a nuisance. A potential problem? Perhaps.

"Light My Fire" filled the apartment as Hal swallowed some more beer and hit the pipe again. On TV, Ford burst through the door of a motel room. It was probably balsa wood. Got to make the hotshot star look good. He leaned forward and laid the pipe back in the ashtray.

And then there was the guy in the porkpie in front of Ford's house. He picked up some computer printouts from the coffee table in front of him and rifled through them. When he'd gotten home, he'd booted up the computer and hacked into the DMV, looking for this porkpie guy. There it was. The license plate he'd put into his PDA was registered to one Eddie Collins. Address on Hollywood Boulevard. He'd googled the name and bingo. A fuckin' private eye. Even more weird, a goddamn actor to boot. The Internet Movie Database had given him a picture, which confirmed that Collins was the guy standing in front of Ford's house. Hal wondered if he'd ever worked with the hot-shot movie star.

He rose from the sofa and sat in front of his laptop. On the IMDB site he linked Mike Ford and Eddie Collins. Yes, indeed. A low-budget horror film from several years back. Hal didn't recognize the title. He printed out the page. Wonder if Collins had ever gotten fucked over by Ford. Probably not. They looked like they were buddies. Would the private eye be guarding Ford's house? Was the guy in the porkpie joining the cast of players in this drama?

Hal pulled another beer from the fridge and listened to

Morrison singing "The End." He giggled and gleefully drummed his fingers on the edge of the table. Damn, this was almost too ironic. He started shifting through the pages of magazines and newspapers, looking for the right letters. Yes, this will be the end, my friend, but first another reminder of the beginning. Hal slipped on a pair of latex gloves, picked up the scissors and started cutting.

Chapter Fifteen

Mavis's husband, Fritz, said she was out in the backyard. That left me at my desk, on the phone, waiting for her. Waiting quite a while, I might add. I bided my time by glancing through my notes and computer pages from the conversation with Mike Ford that morning.

Then I heard background noise on the phone, and Mavis said, "Hey, what's up?"

"What were you doing back there, burying the evidence?"

"Picking tomatoes. And a crack like that just might blow your chances of getting some."

"Damn, a BLT does sound pretty good, I must admit."

"What can I do for you, boss man?"

"I need you to pick up a couple things before you come in tomorrow morning."

"What?"

"An inexpensive digital camera and a cell phone."

"Eddie, don't tell me you've lost your cell phone?"

"No, no, nothing like that. It's for Tired Reggie."

"Who in the heck is Tired Reggie?"

I gave her the *Reader's Digest* condensed version. Our stint together in Korea and how I'd found him on the Santa Monica Pier and was going to put him on the payroll on a trial basis.

"You're going to do what?"

"He needs a leg up. I've got some things he can do. Surveillance on Mike Ford's house, for one. That's why I need the camera and the cell phone."

Silence on the other end of the line. "Look, kiddo, I don't know if this is going to work, but I owe him."

She finally said, "Okay, I'll go to Best Buy and get one of those disposable phones, the ones you just buy minutes for."

"That's the ticket. Put all the numbers in it. Office, my cell, yours."

"Hold it. I'm not that kind of girl. I've got to meet the guy before I give him my phone number."

"You will."

"Does he even know how to use them?"

"Yeah, he had one of each a while back. They got ripped off. I'll pay you back in the morning. When are you coming in?"

"You name it."

"I've got a noon call at Disney. I want to get him settled in at Mike's before that."

"Eight o'clock all right?"

"Perfect. See you then. Oh, and just a couple of tomatoes will do."

I heard a snort before I broke the connection. I went into my apartment, grabbed a beer and returned to the desk. A movie poster of Bogie and Bacall in *To Have and Have Not* stared down at me as I leaned back in my chair and sipped from the beer, wondering if I was doing the right thing.

On the ride in from Santa Monica I'd laid out the

whole plan in front of Reggie. At first he was reluctant, but I said we'd do this on a trial basis, see if it worked out. I told him I didn't want to pressure him into anything, but that I hadn't forgotten that night in Korea. I said I'd try and help him get back on his feet. There was a sense of pride within him that made him hesitant, but he finally agreed to give it a shot.

I found a motel with long-term rates that had a kitchenette with a microwave. I paid for a week, Reggie showered and we headed out for a Walmart and got him outfitted with some clothes. The laundry bag he'd picked up at the 7-Eleven provided little help. After Walmart, we stopped at a Ralph's and stocked up on basic foodstuffs for his kitchenette. I reminded him that he'd have to parcel the food out over a few days. He nodded and said no problem, but I could tell the provisions were awfully tempting. Probably more food than he'd seen in one place for months. I gave him some cash and left him with the television on. I told him I'd pick him up in the morning. He shook my hand, held it for a long moment, and then gave me a bear hug. That alone was enough to make me think I was doing the right thing.

I sipped from my beer and went back to the notes Mike had printed out that morning. I had to hand it to him; he'd put together a pretty impressive *résumé*. He'd done twenty-eight pictures, directing eight of them. Given the number of people who'd worked with him, the task of finding someone with enough of a grudge to send those threatening letters began to look daunting.

I tilted my chair back and looked at the *Red Desert*

computer pages. Sometimes the film community in this town becomes very small. The fact that Mike Ford, Jack Boylston and Mickey Patterson had all worked on the same picture was coincidental, but not impossible. But were they linked in some way beyond this movie? Had something happened out in Barstow other than a movie being shot?

I looked at the cast list. Ford, Boylston, Patterson. I vaguely recognized a couple of the other names, but couldn't offhand recall why. My eyes landed on a character listed as "Hank Barton" played by one Whit Baxter. The name "Whit" jumped out at me. I'd heard it recently. I gazed up at Bogie and Bacall, trying to remember when and where. Then it hit me. In my conversation yesterday with Jack he'd mentioned that his friend Jimmy Whitmore had a stage name. Whit something. He said he couldn't remember the last name.

I pulled my Rolodex in front of me and found the Boylstons' phone number. Helen picked up after three rings.

"Hello, Helen? It's Eddie Collins calling."

"Why, Mr. Collins, how nice to hear from you."

"Is Jack there?"

"He's out in the back trying to fix the screen door on the garage. It's not going very well. He's already hit his thumb twice."

"I need to talk to him about our conversation yesterday. You think you could get him for me?"

"Oh, my yes. It's probably a good idea. He's about ready to throw the hammer out in the alley. Hold on."

She put the receiver down. I could hear her hollering at Jack. After his muffled reply she picked up the phone again. "He told me he wasn't going to wander off anymore. I don't know whether or not to believe him. Maybe I should put him on a leash." She laughed and I had to grin at the image. "Here he is."

"Collins? You think I'm lost again? I'm talkin' to you, ain't I?"

"That you are, Jack. Listen, yesterday you said your friend Jimmy Whitmore had a stage name. Whit something. Remember that?"

"Hell, yes. The union said Jimmy Whitmore was too close to James Whitmore. You know, the guy that was in that Shawshank picture?"

"Right. I know who you mean. What last name did he use with Whit?"

There was silence on the end of the line for a moment. "Ah, lemme think."

"Was it Baxter?"

"By God, that's it! How'd you know that?"

"He was in *Red Desert* with you, right?"

"Yeah, he was. I think he forgot about it, though. Wish I could do the same damn thing."

"Do you happen to know his address?"

"He's over on Mildred."

"What's the house number?"

"Hell, I don't know. I never look at the number."

"No problem. I'll find it."

"What do you want with him?"

"I need to talk to him about Mike Ford."

"Hah! Good luck with that."

"Well, I'll give it a try. I'll let you get back to your screen door."

"Yeah, okay. I ain't completely broke my hand yet."

He hung up the phone. I flipped Rolodex cards to the Fs and he picked up after two rings.

"Mike, it's Eddie."

"Hey, what's goin' on?"

"What can you tell me about Whit Baxter?"

After a long pause and an audible sigh he said, "Oh Christ, I forgot about him when we were talking this morning."

"He was also in *Red Desert*, right?"

"He was. And he got into some trouble when we were shooting the picture."

"What kind of trouble?"

"He had a dustup with some Marines one night."

"Hold it. Marines in Barstow?"

"Yeah. There's a Marine Corps Logistics Base outside of town. We had permission to shoot some scenes on their property. We also used some of the GIs as extras. Baxter was in a bar one night and got into a fight with some of them over a local Hispanic girl. Later that night she wandered into the police station claiming she was raped."

"By Baxter?"

"No, by a couple of the Marines. They denied it. The brass stepped in and along with the local cops put the squeeze on her. She eventually changed her story."

"To what?"

"That it was Baxter. Said she was confused. She was

high on something, so who the hell knows what the truth was."

"Did they do a DNA test?"

"They did. Baxter didn't deny having sex with her, but he said it was consensual. So did the Marines."

"How'd it wind up?"

"The Marine Corps pours a hell of a lot of money into that town. I think they pressured the local cops and the woman. It was her word against Baxter."

"What happened to him?"

"We posted bail for him and they let him finish the shoot. After we went back to LA he went on trial. I guess he wound up doing a year or something."

"So now he's got an axe to grind with you?"

"How do you figure?"

"Not going to bat for him? Leaving him out there?"

"Well, hell, Eddie, there wasn't much I or the production could do for him. He admitted being with the woman. We bailed him out."

"Ever heard about him since then?"

"No. Why?"

"Boylston says he lives out in Venice. I'll see if I can track him down. In the meantime, I've got somebody to watch your house."

"Really? Who?"

"Reggie Benson. An old friend of mine from the Army days. You think there's any problem with him squatting down in the brush across the street from you?"

"Nah, I don't think so. The lot belongs to the Ellsworths around the corner. I doubt if they ever bother to get to the back end of it."

"Good. I'll put him there with a camera. If the guy drops something else in your mail slot, he'll be on film."

"Sounds good. Look, if you need any help on my end through my production company, Lois Moore is the one to call. It might be easier for her to get a headshot or phone number from an agent."

I jotted down the name and said I'd check in with him later. After I hung up I called Reggie's motel room and he answered in a timid-sounding voice.

"It's Eddie. How you doin?"

"I'm good. Having my own room is pretty far-out."

"Got everything you need?"

"Yup, yup, think so. I watched a movie and had some microwave popcorn. Stuff's like cardboard."

"Tell you what. We'll catch a flick one of these days and have some of the real thing."

"Okay." There was a pause on the line and I could hear the television in the background. "Hey, Eddie?"

"Yeah?"

"You sure you wanna do this?"

"Of course I am. Aren't you?"

"I guess so. I just don't want you to think...well, you know."

"Hey, listen, Reggie. Let's just take it a day at a time, okay?"

"All right."

"I'll pick you up about ten o'clock. Get you situated over at Ford's place."

"Okay. Kind of like bein' back in the Army, huh,

Eddie? Pullin' guard duty."

"That's it exactly. Get a good night's sleep, all right?"

"Gonna do that. Been awhile since I've had my own bed."

"Enjoy it. See you in the morning."

I hung up and walked back into the apartment to get another beer. The fan was going full blast, but the room was still hot. Reggie was going to have to be out in this heat tomorrow. Could he do it? If I got hung up at Disney, Mavis could always pick him up.

Let the experiment begin. A day at a time.

Chapter Sixteen

Los Angelinos tend to forget that we basically live in a desert. Water is scarce. The owner of the tattoo slash smoke shop across from my building on the Boulevard obviously hadn't gotten the news. I stood on my balcony with coffee cup in hand watching him hose down the sidewalk in front of his establishment. Several stars on the Hollywood Walk of Fame were getting a bath, so maybe he was providing a public service. Hopefully his water bill would precipitate an introduction to a push broom.

Thinking of living in a desert caused me to recall my phone conversation yesterday regarding Whit Baxter, aka Jimmy Whitmore. Mike had said the guy did time in Barstow after working on *Red Desert*. That fact alone would be motive for holding a grudge, but why had he waited all these years? And would Mike Ford be the proper target? If I could jumpstart his memory regarding the incident, Jack Boylston could give more information. As could Mickey Patterson, despite being very young when the movie shoot occurred.

I stepped back inside the apartment and shut the doors against the heat and the smell of smoke from the ongoing fires. Mavis's presence could be heard in the outer office.

"Eddie?"

"Yeah, be right there," I said, as I rinsed my coffee cup.

Last night I'd rummaged around in my closet and found a small knapsack and a couple of insulated thermos bottles. I pulled them out of the fridge and filled them with cold water. Reggie would no doubt need them today. With the knapsack over my shoulder I pawed through the beaded doorway and saw a small paper sack sitting on my desk. Inside were three large tomatoes. "Are these Burpee Big Boys?"

Mavis poked her head into my office. "How do you know what Burpee Big Boys are?"

"I come from a long line of tomato growers."

She gave me one of her more attractive sneers and said, "Yeah, right. I'll lay you ten to one they'll turn to mush in that so-called lair of yours back there."

"You're on. Did you get the camera and phone?" She ducked back to her desk and reappeared with a plastic bag from Best Buy. Inside were a small Canon and a cell phone.

"I charged the phone up overnight and put the numbers in it. Mine too."

"Great." I sat down at my desk, pulled the camera and phone from the bag and looked at the receipt.

"Fritz said if I get any weird phone calls from this Tired Reggie guy, he's going to come over here and give you what for."

I looked up at her. "Tell me he's kidding." Fritz is a burly bus driver and has been known to bench press his weight as easily as lifting a bag of dryer lint.

"Actually he was...sort of."

"Well, you can relax. Reggie is a pussycat."

She sat in a chair in front of my desk. "Are you sure you're doing the right thing with him?"

"Not entirely. But we'll see how it goes." I flipped open the phone and looked at the display.

"Since he's now on the payroll, I suppose it's out of the question to ask for a raise."

"You can always ask."

I glanced up at her and saw the squint in her eyes and the pursing of her lips. "Mavis, I don't know if it's going to be something long-term. Reggie can help me out on this Mike Ford thing. Maybe down the road I can get him some kind of a job, something more permanent. He doesn't even have a driver's license. Hopefully I can work out a deal where he can find a cheap apartment and get back on track with his life."

I scrunched up the plastic bag, then grabbed my checkbook and wrote her a check. When I handed it to her, she was no longer squinting and pursing.

"It was quite a few years ago, but I can remember it like it was yesterday. The look in that staff sergeant's face when he came at me with a knife. I don't know if I'd be sitting here talking to you if it weren't for Reggie. I can't just buy him some fish tacos and walk away."

Mavis looked at me for a long moment. "He isn't the only pussycat." I tossed the scrunched-up plastic bag at her and she caught it on the fly. "So when do I get to meet him?"

"Maybe later today. If it gets too damn hot out there sitting in the brush you may have to go and pick him up."

"Okay, leave me Ford's address," she said, as she got up

and went back into her office.

I took the tomatoes back to my fridge, came back and stuck the camera and the cell phone in the knapsack, popped a porkpie on my head and walked into the front office. The aroma of fresh coffee filled the room as Mavis sat at her desk checking the eBay site, something she does without fail every morning.

"Did you see the name of that Baxter guy?"

"Yup."

"He's an actor. I need an address for him on Mildred out in Venice. Whit Baxter is an alias. His real name is Jimmy Whitmore."

"I'll do a Google search first, and go from there."

"Mike said his production company could probably help you find him."

"How they going to do that?"

"They'll call SAG, tell them Parkwood Productions is looking for Whit Baxter. They've got a project he might be right for. What agent is he with? Then they call the agent and tell them to fax over a picture and *résumé*. It should have the guy's phone number and address on it."

"Neat."

I pointed to the slip of paper I'd put on her desk. "That Lois Moore there is Mike's assistant. She should be able to help you."

"Got it." She sipped from her coffee cup. "So you're at Disney until when?"

"Dunno for sure. Hopefully mid-afternoon. I think it's just a table-read." I handed her another slip of paper. "Here's Mike's address. In Los Feliz, north of Franklin. I'll give you a buzz later."

"Okie-dokie, boss man."

"Thanks for the Burpees. I put them in the fridge."

"No, no, no. They'll lose their flavor that way."

"Oops," I said as I started back to my apartment.

She shook her head and waved me toward the door. "Never mind. I'll take care of them. You better get going."

"Yes, ma'am," I said as I opened the door. "Maybe you do need that raise."

I think the door was shut before she heard me.

Chapter Seventeen

Not even ten o'clock yet, and already sweat was breaking out on the back of my neck. News from my car radio said the fires were still burning up near Lake Arrowhead and Big Bear Lake. Only forty percent contained and moving to the west. Reggie was not going to have a comfortable day.

When I knocked on the door of his motel room, he pulled it open and I had to look twice. He'd shaved his beard. Yesterday he'd told me he was going to trim it, but I hadn't expected this. He wore a green tee shirt and camo cargo pants. The new hiking shoes we'd bought were on his feet.

"Hi, Eddie. Come on in."

"So you fell in love with that razor and couldn't stop yourself, huh?"

He grinned and swiped a hand across his chin. "Ah, I got tired of the dang thing. Too hot anyway."

I handed him the knapsack with the thermos bottles. "There's cold water in here. You're probably going to need it."

"Got a couple of bottles from the vending machine too." He took the knapsack and opened his mini-fridge. "Made myself some sandwiches. Pretty good ham here. And some turkey." He began stuffing provisions into the bag.

"All right, you look like you're good to go." I reached

into a pocket of the knapsack and pulled out the camera and the cell phone. "Mavis put all the phone numbers in here for you."

"Who's Mavis?"

"My secretary. If it gets too hot out there later she'll come and pick you up."

"Boy, secretary and everything. You're an important dude." He popped me on the shoulder and flashed a big grin. It was nice to see him in an upbeat mood.

I handed him the camera and phone. "You're sure you know how to use these things?"

He flipped the phone open and started pushing keys. "Yup, yup. Here's the menu, contact list." He pushed more buttons. "Yup, there ya go. Hey, this has got a camera in it. Didn't have to buy the other one."

"I don't think those phone cameras take very good pictures. If you see someone outside Ford's house, we need a real clear image."

"Yup, yup." He stowed the camera and phone in the bag and slapped a cap on his head. "Let's do it."

I pulled open the door, stepped out on the balcony and looked at him. "Didn't you forget something?"

"What?"

I held up my car key and turned my wrist. "The door."

"Oh, shit." He patted his pockets, looked around the room and finally picked up a card key from the dresser. "Well, you see if they made a key, a guy'd remember."

"I'm with you there."

He pulled the door closed behind him and jiggled the handle to make sure it was shut.

"Haven't had to lock a door lately."

I grinned and popped him on the shoulder. "Get used to it."

***

Reggie seemed to know who Mike Ford was. He'd seen a film or two of his years ago, but couldn't remember their names. I told him about Janice Ebersole's death, the two letters Mike had received and why he was staking out the front of his house.

I called Mike on the way. He said he was home, but had to leave soon for meetings. As I pulled into the driveway I'd parked in yesterday, he came out of the house to meet us. He carried a briefcase and had a blazer draped over one arm. He locked the door behind him, walked up to us and stuck out his hand to Reggie.

"Morning. I'm Mike Ford. Reggie, isn't it?"

"That's me," Reggie said, taking his hand. "Reggie Benson. Sorry about your loss, sir."

"Thanks." He gestured to me. "So I hear you know the private eye here from the Army."

"We were MPs together. In Korea."

Mike gestured to the brush across the street. "You going to be all right in there?"

"I think so, sir."

"I don't foresee the neighbors giving you any trouble. Matter of fact, they shouldn't even know you're there." He reached into his shirt pocket and pulled out one of his business cards. "But if you run into any problems, give me a call."

"Okay," Reggie said. He looked at the card, apparently

not quite believing that he was standing here talking to one of Hollywood's major stars.

"And you're over at Disney, right, Eddie?"

"Yeah. I'll talk to the Patterson kid. See what he says."

"Good. Well, I better saddle up. Glad to meet you, Reggie. Try to stay cool. At least you'll be in shade."

"Yup, yup, it'll be okay," he replied.

Mike walked off to his garage. I looked up and down the street for any vehicles, joggers, or walkers. Nottingham was empty. I led Reggie across the street. He found a place and crawled up the incline, grabbing onto some exposed roots to help him. When he got to the top he looked back at me, a big grin on his face.

"Remember your first General Order, Eddie?"

"Haven't got a clue."

"Me neither. I was tryin' to think of it last night. No dice."

The first General Order was something every GI had to drum into his head, especially when he was walking guard duty. "Today it's trying not to get your ass bitten by the bugs. You got that repellant we bought, right?"

"Yup, got it. I'll see ya later, Eddie." He flipped me a salute and walked into the brush.

I backed my car out and headed down Nottingham. Reggie had already disappeared. So far, day one of the experiment looked successful.

Chapter Eighteen

For the life of him Hal couldn't understand how Victor Mature warranted a star on the Hollywood Walk of Fame. As he stood looking down at the actor's pentagram, he recalled Mature having been quoted as saying, "I'm no actor, and I've got 64 pictures to prove it." To Hal's way of thinking, *Samson and Delilah* and the other sword and sandal epics Mature was known for proved the point. Nevertheless, there he was, Victor Mature, embedded in the sidewalk, enshrined in fame.

Hal slapped his thigh with his clipboard, shook his head in disgust and continued down the boulevard, dodging the endless parade of camera-toting tourists and gawkers. No doubt Mike Ford also had his own star. He didn't know where it was, and he damn sure wasn't going to look for it.

Based on the IMDB credits Hal had looked up, there was no way Eddie Collins would merit a star. But he did have an office on Hollywood Boulevard. Hal checked his clipboard. And here it was. He stood in front of the building and glanced over at the hole-in-the-wall hot dog stand to the right.

He pulled the door open and stepped inside. A directory on the wall to his left confirmed Collins Investigations as being on the fifth floor. He ran his finger over the entries on the directory, looking for other fifth floor occupants. The Elite Talent Agency, *Pecs and Abs* magazine, and a doctor with a Russian-sounding name shared the floor with Collins.

A single-car elevator was at the end of the corridor, a stairway on the left. To the right at the end of a short hallway a steel door sat under an exit sign. Hal opened it. Three steps led to a landing and what appeared to be a parking lot. He reached around and turned the knob. Locked from the outside. No problem. It could be picked. He propped the door open with his clipboard, walked down the steps and saw three parking spaces, only one of them occupied. The vehicle was a Volkswagen, not the one belonging to Collins. The parking spaces opened onto an alley.

He climbed back up the three stairs, retrieved his clipboard and swung the door shut behind him. Back at the elevator, he pressed the "up" button and heard the groan of the car descending. Behind him, the front door opened. A young black woman in tattered denim shorts and a tie-died halter-top entered. She wore sunglasses and a battered straw hat. As she passed Hal she nodded and headed for the stairs. Hal watched her disappear upward. Nice butt. Probably one of the talent agency's clients.

The elevator door opened and he stepped inside and pressed the number five button. With a jerk the car began its ascent. This was the only address he could find for Collins. He had to make sure he didn't live somewhere else. Hal looked at the shipping invoice on his clipboard and adjusted his cap. No wonder the model took the stairs. She'd be past her prime by the time the elevator got to the fifth floor.

Another jerk and the car stopped on five. After a few seconds, the door creaked open and Hal started to exit. A guy suddenly bumped into him. He wore one of the loudest Hawaiian shirts Hal had ever seen, parrots and egrets clamoring for space. Earrings dangled from the guy's lobes, skin-tight red leather pants covered his legs and a large Panama hat was perched on his head.

"Oh, sorry, honey," the guy said. "Didn't think anybody was on this relic."

"No problem," Hal said. He watched the guy prance into the elevator car and push the down button, looking back to eye him from head to toe. The door closed and jerked its way down. Definitely not the Russian doctor, Hal thought.

Collins Investigations was on the left side of the hall, opposite the doctor's office and the stairwell. Next to the doctor's office was an unmarked door. Hal turned the knob. It was unlocked. He pushed it open and found a light switch. The closet contained an upright vacuum cleaner and a small metal shelf on which sat various cleaning supplies. He shut the light off and quietly pulled the door closed.

Hal gave another tug to the bill of his cap. It and the shirt he wore were from a shipping company. He'd ripped them off the wardrobe department of a commercial he'd shot a few months back. The invoice on his clipboard was fake. He opened the door to Collins Investigations. An attractive blond woman sat behind a desk, talking on the telephone. She glanced at him and held up one finger as he closed the door behind him. On the far side of the small office a door led to another room. Was his apartment back there somewhere? The telephone conversation ended and the woman turned to him.

"Can I help you?"

"I've got a delivery for Eddie Collins."

"You've got the right place."

He looked at the clipboard. "Ah, well, I was expecting a residence. This is only an office, right?"

"Also a residence. What's the delivery?"

Hal glanced at the invoice. "Perishables, from Wellington Imports. I wasn't sure I got the right place, so I left it on the truck. I'll be right back up with it."

Hal backed out of the office, shut the door and headed down the stairs. The blonde had a suspicious look on her face. He better not be caught waiting for that prehistoric elevator. Another young woman, this one in heels and a mini skirt, teetered her way up the stairs. Hal said "Hi" and kept moving. He walked out of the stairwell and back onto Hollywood Boulevard. He removed the invoice from his clipboard, ripped it up and threw it in a wire trash barrel and threaded his way through the crush of tourists on the street. So Collins Investigations was not only office but also home. Interesting.

Chapter Nineteen

The only new cast member at the *Before the Beginning* table-read was a stunning redhead by the name of Beryl Devon. She was playing an assistant DA and was supposed to be the nemesis of Benny Bonnano and Percy Shank. I recognized her from a few things she'd done. Her allure and professionalism were wonderful assets. They were offset, however, by the script from which we read. It had all the humor of a train wreck. At these table-reads the writers and producers usually sit off to the side, following along with the script. When one of them laughs, they all look at each other for a moment and then join in. Monkey see, monkey do.

Today the only sound in this studio on the Disney lot was the hum of the air conditioning. I put forth my best effort in trying to be humorous as Officer Danforth, but it was a tough slog. I didn't have enough lines, for one thing. And the few remaining were written on paper that could be better served by wrapping fish.

When we finished, the writers and producers quietly closed their scripts and huddled with the director in the corner of the room. After a few minutes they somberly filed from the studio and the stage manager announced that we were wrapped for the day. The second AD would be notifying us with tomorrow's call-time.

The stage manager walked over to Mickey Patterson

and Denny Stinson, leaned over them and said something I couldn't hear, then walked off. The two stars sat staring at each other as if they'd just buried a dear friend. After a moment they stood up and started to walk toward the door. I caught up with Mickey as he walked to his trailer.

"Hey, Mickey, got a minute?"

He turned and saw me. "You going to start ragging on me again?"

"Not unless you had anything to do with hiring those writers."

"Oh, my God, can you believe it? There's a couple of Emmys in that group that need to be returned." He reached up and stuck a key into the lock on the trailer's door. "What do you want, Collins? The office is supposed to call me in a bit. See what we can do about this mess."

"I just need to ask you a couple of questions."

"What about?"

"A film you did called *Red Desert*."

Mickey froze for a moment and turned to look at me. "Man, there's a golden oldie. What about it?"

"You got air conditioning in there?"

He stared at me for a bit, then opened the door. "Come on."

I followed him inside. It wasn't a big trailer, but it was a welcome retreat from the heat. There was a small bedroom at the end of a short hallway, a bathroom half way down on the right. A kitchenette, table, and two sofas occupied the rest of the trailer. Mickey gestured for me to have a seat. I pulled out a chair and sat at the table as he opened the door of the refrigerator. He grabbed a bottled energy drink. "You want something?"

"I don't suppose you've got a beer in there?"

"What do you think? I'm a minor, Collins."

"Oh, yeah, right. How could I forget? Give me one of those things you've got."

He grabbed another bottle and tossed it to me. I twisted the plastic cap and watched him kick off his sneakers and sit on one end of the smaller sofa. He tucked his feet underneath him.

"You actually watched that movie?"

"I did. You remember Mike Ford?"

"Sure. Directing and starring as the Pecos Kid." He made an elaborate and make-believe gesture of drawing his pistol and shooting the bad guy. Seeing I was not amused, he took a healthy hit off his drink, then suddenly pulled his feet out from under him and lunged to the edge of the sofa.

"Speaking of which, didn't I just read about him the other day? A burglary or something?"

"Somebody broke into his house and stole his Oscar. His girlfriend Janice Ebersole was found dead in the swimming pool."

"No shit? Murdered?"

"LAPD hasn't ruled on it yet."

"Man, that sucks." His sincerity sounded as flat as the lines he'd been reading a few minutes ago.

"How well did you get to know Ford when you were shooting the picture?"

"As much as an actor gets to know a director. I was just a kid, though, so I mean, we didn't hang out or anything."

"You get along with him?"

Mickey drank from his bottle and thought for a minute. "Far as I can remember. Why?"

"He's received a couple of strange letters in the last few days. Almost threatening."

Mickey got up from the sofa and sat across from me at the table. He leaned in on his elbows, his eyes wide open, grinning. "Now I get it. The other day somebody told me you were a PI. I said they were full of shit. Is it true, Collins? You a gumshoe? Like Sam Spade, trench coat, bottle of booze in the desk drawer, all that stuff?" He sucked on his plastic bottle and glanced at me sideways.

I took a pull from my bottle of what appeared to be flavored water and looked at him. He had this idiotic smirk on his face almost as if he wanted me to tell him how clever he was. I wasn't going to bite.

"It pays the bills. I don't have a hit sitcom like some guys."

He gestured to my porkpie. "So that's the reason for the Popeye Doyle hat, huh?"

"Some people wear baseball caps. Others might settle for a Tam o'Shanter or a Stetson. You, Mickey, I figure for a beanie with a propeller. Now why don't you knock off this Pee-wee Herman bullshit? If you want to be funny, go over and stick your head into your writers' room."

He leaned back and put up his hands, palms out. "Okay, okay, man. Chill. I'm just jerking your chain."

He finished his drink and flipped the empty bottle in the direction of the trash. He wasn't even in the vicinity, so he got up and retrieved the bottle and disposed of it, then reseated himself.

"You think I had something to do with these letters, Collins? Kinda fishing, aren't you?"

"I don't know. You tell me." I pulled the copies from my pocket and handed the first one to him. "This was mailed to him. The wording strike you as a little coincidental?"

He opened the letter and read. "Before the Beginning There Was Me." He looked up. "That's fuckin' weird, ain't it?"

I handed him the second letter. "This one was left on the shelf where his Oscar sat."

He looked at it and shook his head. "Some nut job."

"You sure you haven't got an axe to grind with Mike Ford?"

"That's crazy. Christ, I hardly got to know the guy. I was a kid, still putting Clearasil on my zits. I haven't seen him since."

"You don't know where he lives?"

"Don't have a clue."

"Never worked with him again?"

"Like I said, I haven't seen him since. Except for the films and stuff he's done." Mickey ran his hands through his greasy hair and got up to open the refrigerator. "One more?" I shook my head and he pulled out another bottle and sat in his chair.

"Why would I have any kind of an axe to grind with Mike Ford? I mean, look, I've got a show. I'm making money. Life's pretty good."

I sipped from my bottle and acknowledged that he had

a point. "You remember someone else that worked on the picture? Guy by the name of Jack Boylston? He played a stagecoach driver."

Mickey picked at some acne on his chin as he thought. "Yeah, vaguely. Little wiry guy I think."

"You ever witness any beef between him and Ford?"

He shook his head. "Nah, it seemed to be a pretty copacetic group from what I remember."

"What about a guy by the name of Whit Baxter?"

Mickey took his hand from his chin and looked at me. "Man, who you been talking to?"

"Why? What do you mean?"

"You're digging up some dirt now."

"What kind of dirt?"

He twisted the cap off the plastic bottle, drank, then replaced the top and shook his head. "Baxter got into trouble with the Marines. It was a goddamn mess."

"I heard he was charged with raping some local girl."

"Yeah, I guess so."

"What do you mean, you 'guess so?'"

He slurped from the plastic bottle and set it down. He had an uncomfortable look on his face. "There were rumors floating around the set."

"What kind of rumors?"

"Aw, I don't know. That he didn't do it. Someone else did."

"Some Marines, right?"

"Yeah, maybe. Maybe somebody else."

"Who?"

"I don't know. For crissakes, I was just a kid. I wasn't

privy to everything going on."

Both of us jumped when the phone rang. Mickey rose from the table and picked up the receiver. "Yeah?" He paused and looked at me. "Okay. I'm on the way." He hung up the phone and began to slip his sneakers on. "That was the office. The suits want to talk to us. Gotta go, Collins."

I finished my energy drink, put the letters back in my pocket and stood up from the table. "If you remember anything else, let me know."

"Yeah, I will. But you better talk to Baxter."

"That's my plan." I walked to the door and opened it. "I'll see you tomorrow. Let's hope your writers burn some midnight oil."

"They damn sure better. And, hey. It's a cool hat, man. Really."

I ceremoniously doffed the porkpie to him and stepped back out into the heat. Part of what Patterson had told me wasn't surprising. It'd be unlikely for a kid to come up with a vendetta like this. And he was right. He didn't have much of a motive. But what he did have was the memory of rumors. Ugly things, rumors. What hadn't Mike Ford told me? Was there some way to pry more information from the muddled mind of Jack Boylston about what went on out there in the desert around Barstow? What would Whit Baxter tell me?

Unanswered questions pressed down on me like the unrelenting sun here on the Disney lot. As I pulled my cell phone from my pocket to call Reggie, I suddenly felt hampered by this silly-ass sitcom. I had more important things to do.

His cell began to ring. Maybe Tired Reggie was going to prove more useful than I had originally thought.

Chapter Twenty

Reggie didn't look the worse for wear as he grabbed an exposed tree root and slid down the embankment across from Ford's house. He pulled the car door open and I handed him a cold bottle of water.

"You okay, Reggie?"

"Yeah, I'm good. Glad you got air conditioning."

He downed most of the water and pointed to the front of Ford's house. "See, there's those phone books I told you about."

Two thick directories encased in plastic lay on the small bench under Ford's mail slot. When I'd called Reggie after my talk with Mickey Patterson, he said he'd taken several pictures. One of them captured a van and a guy delivering telephone books. He'd also gotten a shot of the mailman and a few other vehicles and pedestrians passing by the house.

"You got a computer we can download the pictures to, right?"

"That's Mavis's department," I said as I pulled into the driveway, turned around and headed back down Nottingham.

"So I'm gonna meet your secretary, huh?"

"Yup. She's looking forward to it."

He shook his head. "Oh, boy."

"What's the matter?"

"Aw, you know, Eddie, I ain't been around the ladies too much lately."

"No girlfriend?"

"You kiddin?'"

"Well, you don't have to worry about Mavis. She won't bite. Besides, she's married."

"That's good." He tapped the empty water bottle against his knee in time with Dry Branch Fire Squad coming through the car's speakers.

"I like your tunes," he said.

I upped the volume a tad as I pulled onto Franklin. We headed toward the office and I glanced over at him as he watched the Los Feliz mansions gliding past. He looked almost boyish. Knowing my secretary like I do, that quality would more than likely jump-start her motherly instinct.

***

Mavis didn't sound very maternal as we pushed open the door of Collins Investigations. We heard her voice coming from the little bathroom alcove. Some unfortunate soul on the other end of a telephone conversation was receiving both barrels.

"Look, Manny, or whatever the hell your name is, you told me two days ago you'd have somebody here. This faucet keeps dripping, my water bill keeps going up, and you still tell me you're on the way. Are you riding a burro from Encino or what?"

She paused for Manny's reply and Reggie looked at me. "Thought you said she didn't bite?"

"She doesn't. Those are just nips."

I put the digital camera on her desk and picked up the day's mail. Mavis stood in the doorway of her bathroom cubicle, hand cocked on one hip. I knew the pose. Manny didn't know how lucky he was not to be receiving this tirade in person.

"I come in at eight a.m. If nine o'clock rolls around and you're not here, I'm turning you in to whoever the heck made a mistake by giving you your license." Pause. "I'm not hostile. Hostility starts tomorrow morning at nine o'clock."

Manny's answer must have been satisfactory. She said "Okay," broke the connection and turned, startled to see me.

"Oh. Hi, Eddie." She stepped into the office, her surprise increasing when she saw Reggie standing to her right.

"Reggie Benson, meet Mavis, the other half of Collins Investigations."

"So you're the Tired Reggie I've been hearing about? Nice to meet you."

"Hi. Eddie told you 'bout my nickname, huh?"

"He did. Being around him sometimes makes me tired too, Reggie." She walked behind her desk and slammed the phone down on its base.

"What's with the plumber?" I asked.

"Two weeks ago he was in here and didn't fix the problem."

"Did you pay him?"

"Yes. Money down the drain, I guess. No pun intended."

A little grin appeared on Reggie's face. Good plan, I

thought. Appreciate her jokes, intended or not.

"Anything else exciting happen?" I said.

She handed me a slip of paper. "Here's the house number for Whit Baxter."

I slipped it into my notebook. "Reggie got some shots outside Ford's house. We can download them, right?"

"No problem." She opened her middle desk drawer and took out a small cord still wrapped with a plastic twist. "Did you fry out in that heat, Reggie? Heck of a way to start a new job."

"It wasn't too bad, ma'am."

"Mavis. No 'ma'am' around here." She unwrapped the cord and plugged one end into the computer and the other into the camera.

"Let me get a beer," I said as I started back to my apartment. "You got a cold soda for Reggie in that inner sanctum of yours?"

"Sure thing." She pointed to her alcove. "Help yourself. There's a mini-fridge in there."

I walked back to my apartment, wondering why I've never received permission to enter that sanctum sanctorum of hers. I rescued a cold beer from isolation. When I got back to the front office they were looking at the pictures downloading. I set my glass on the desk and peered over Mavis's shoulder. She pulled an apple-shaped coaster from her belly drawer and set my beer on it.

The digital images filled the screen. Mavis enlarged each of them and Reggie provided the commentary. Finally, a shot showed a brown van stopped in front of Ford's house. The vehicle had a sliding door on the passenger side.

Reggie pointed to the picture. "That's the phone directory guy. I took it because he stopped. Looked like he was casing the place. Then I moved downhill and tried to zoom in on the rear license plate. Click on the next image." Mavis did so. "Aw, damn, I think I got a leaf or something in the frame. But you can see some of it."

"Can you enlarge that?" I said. She clicked the mouse. Most of the image was blurred, but some of the numbers became visible. "What is that? '7NG?'"

"Looks like it to me," Mavis replied, as she jotted the digits on a pad of paper.

"He comes back down the hill," Reggie said. He shifted his weight from one foot to the other and pointed at the screen. "Here. This is good. The plate in this one is at the end of the front bumper on the driver's side. Got a real good shot."

Mavis clicked on another picture of the van, again opposite Ford's front entrance, this time the front of the van facing Reggie's camera. She enlarged the image and the plate became more visible. She leaned closer to the screen.

"I can only make out the last two digits. Looks like they're '6L.'" She put the digits on the pad of paper. "'7NG, blank, blank, 6L.'" She looked up at both of us. "I hate to spoil the party, guys, but you've only got a partial plate. And what's the significance of somebody delivering phone books?"

"Good question," Reggie said. "But click on the next few pictures."

She did and we saw the guy getting out of his van, putting the directories on the bench with his back to us, and then catching him as he came back to the door of the vehicle.

"There! See that? He's wearing latex gloves," Reggie said.

"So?" Mavis replied.

"I delivered yellow pages for a while in San Diego. I never wore latex gloves."

Mavis leaned in and looked at the image. "Wait a minute. I've seen this guy."

"Where?" I said.

"He came in here this morning, after you guys left."

She told us about the Wellington Imports deliveryman who didn't deliver anything. We stared at the image in front of us until the phone broke us out of our reverie. Mavis picked it up and handed the receiver to me.

"It's Mike Ford."

"Yeah?" I listened, said "Right," and replaced the handset. I pointed at the picture of the yellow pages deliverer.

"I think I know why that guy's wearing those latex gloves."

Chapter Twenty-One

Mike's phone call informed me he'd gotten another cryptic note, this one again not mailed, but dropped in his mail slot. From the pictures Reggie had taken, the guy in the van appeared to be the culprit. He'd had his back to the camera when he laid the directories on the bench. All he had to do was lean over and slip it through the slot. He had the latex gloves on. No prints.

The note was being faxed to us. While we waited, Mavis did a computer search for Wellington Imports. The company was bogus, the name only meant to gain access to my office.

Reggie sipped from his soda and said, "Eddie, can the cops run a plate even if they don't have all the numbers?"

"I imagine so. It'll result in many more possibles, but with a description of the vehicle, we can narrow it down."

"You got an in with LAPD?"

"Matter of fact I do. Lieutenant Charlie Rivers. We go back a ways."

Mavis stepped into the office with a handful of photo paper.

The phone chirped and the fax machine started whirring. The crude lettering was the same. I stared at it for a long moment, one sentence jumping off the page at me. There was an added personal twist this time.

"Well, what does it say?" Mavis said.

I handed it to her and finished the beer in my glass. She started reading.

"THE SONG SAYS IT BEST, FORD. WE'VE ONLY JUST BEGUN. TOO BAD YOUR GIRLFRIEND WASN'T A BETTER SWIMMER. PS: ASK YOUR PI BUDDY COLLINS IF HE LIKES THE CARPENTERS."

She handed the note to Reggie. "What's he mean by 'the carpenters?'"

"Richard and Karen," I said. "Back in the seventies they had a hit with 'We've Only Just Begun.'"

"Yeah, I remember them," Reggie said as he looked at the note. "But I don't get it. How come he knows you're friends with Ford?"

"No idea. And how the hell does he know my name, let alone that I'm a PI." I took the note from Reggie. "Any ideas, Mavis?"

She began inserting sheets of photo paper into the printer. "Well, if this jerk is computer-savvy, it's not too difficult. But he'd have to get your name first. From the DMV or someplace."

"Then he'd have to know my car."

"He musta seen you outside his house," Reggie said.

"I made sure the street was empty when I dropped you off and picked you up."

Mavis clicked the computer mouse and the printer started up. "You were there yesterday morning, weren't you? What about then?"

I thought back to being at Ford's house, my car parked

in the driveway. I hadn't noticed anybody out of the ordinary on the street, but then I suddenly remembered something.

"Wait a minute. There was—"

The telephone interrupted my thought. Mavis picked it up and handed the receiver to me. "It's your agent."

I picked up my empty glass and the slip of paper with the license plate numbers. "I'll get it in my office." Reggie followed me and looked at the movie posters on the walls as I picked up the phone. "Morrie, what's going on?"

"Hey, Eddie, I got some bad news and some good news."

"What?"

"Bad news first. They shit-canned that episode of *Before the Beginning* you were booked on."

"They're not going to do it at all?"

"That's what they told me."

"Doesn't surprise me. The script was a disaster."

"The good news is that you're still getting paid for the week."

"That I am glad to hear."

"Now, having said that, I can get you an audition for a TV movie out at Sony. What do you say?"

"Actually, I landed a case, Morrie. I'm pretty tied up."

"*Oy vey* with the gumshoe stuff. All right, call me when you're being an actor again."

He hung up the phone. Reggie peeked through the beaded curtain separating office and apartment.

"Pretty neat, Eddie. You ain't got far to go to work." He sat in a chair facing my desk. "What did you remember out there? Before the phone interrupted you."

I found the card for Charlie Rivers and pulled it off the Rolodex. "Mike and I were standing in front of his place, looking at the brush across the street. This old van came by, going real slow."

"The same one I saw?"

"I can't remember what the damn thing looked like. I was more focused on the brush."

"I'll bet it was him. Now he's gonna start hassling you."

"That's why I've got you to watch my back." I punched in Charlie's cell number. He picked up after three.

"Lieutenant Rivers."

"Charlie, it's Eddie Collins." I put him on speaker so Reggie could hear.

"That the same Collins with the biggest movie collection in Hollywood? Who never invites me over for a beer, some popcorn, a Dirty Harry flick?"

"That's the one," I said. "Listen, I need a favor."

"Why doesn't that surprise me? What's up?"

"I need you to run a plate for me. I've only got a partial. That a problem?"

"Not really, but depending on how partial, you're going to get a whole lot of hits."

"I've got five out of seven numbers."

"That's not too bad. Now tell me how I'm going to classify this as official police business?"

"Lakers tickets? When the season opens?"

"Behind Jack Nicholson?"

"Ah, I don't know about that, Charlie, but as close as I can get."

"That'll work. How soon you need them?"

"In the morning?"

"Hit me with the numbers."

I rattled off the five digits from the piece of paper in front of me.

"Swing by the station about nine. I should have something for you."

"Thanks, Charlie. You're a *mensch*."

"I've been called worse. Later."

I hung up the phone and Reggie looked at me, his eyes wide open.

"Wow, man, that's awesome. If I get busted again, I'm callin' you."

"What'd you get busted for?"

"Loitering, nothing serious."

"Well, let's hope those days are over." I looked at my watch. "We better show those pictures to Mike."

Mavis was done with the printing. I picked up the photos she'd finished. The images were remarkably clear, considering they were zoom shots and enlarged.

"I overheard you talking to Morrie. Sorry about the sitcom."

"A blessing in disguise," I said. "We're heading out. We have to show these to Ford."

"Okay."

"Charlie Rivers is going to have some computer printouts in the morning. You and Reggie can start going through them. Hopefully the list isn't going to be overwhelming. We know the vehicle." I held up the shot of the van from the front angle. "It looks like it's an old

Ford."

Reggie picked up his backpack he'd left by the front door. "Nice to meet you, Mavis. Guess I'll see you in the morning, huh?"

"You bet. It'll give us a chance to get to know each other."

I noticed a little blush on his face as he opened the front door. I started to follow, but Mavis stopped me.

"Eddie, you better take this creep seriously."

"I am, kiddo."

"Not just for yourself."

As she looked at me I detected something on her face that I couldn't remember seeing before. Vulnerability. I walked back to her desk.

"Are you worried because he's been in here?"

"Yes. Since he knows where your office is and he's seen me, how do you know he's not watching?"

I didn't. "You still carry that pepper spray with you, don't you?"

"That isn't much good if he jumps me from behind."

She had me there. "What if we trade parking spaces?" Mavis parks her car in a lot a block away, which, I must admit, at night is not well lit and is off Hollywood Boulevard. I, on the other hand, use one of the assigned spaces for the building.

"You haven't forgotten about Rodney Sullivan, have you?" she said.

No, I hadn't. Several months back I'd been attacked by Sullivan as I was getting out of my car. If it hadn't been for Lenny Daye, my neighbor, I wouldn't be having this conversation. Now that she had brought up Sullivan's name, I realized an attack like that was a possibility, especially with a nut job knowing who and where I was and the fact that she worked for me.

"Tell you what," I said. "There's a parking lot down the street from the Dolby Theatre. Across from Hollywood High. It's got lights all over and there's twenty-four seven security. I know the guy who owns it. I'll rent a space for you. When you usually close up shop here, there's still a lot of activity on the boulevard, right? It should be safer."

"That would make me feel better."

I leaned over and kissed her on the cheek. "You're my right-hand gal, kiddo. Not going to let anything happen to you."

***

Mike Ford sat behind his desk at Parkwood Productions, staring at the 3 x 5 photos Mavis had printed. He shook his head and handed them across the desk.

"The guy doesn't look familiar, Eddie."

"How about the van? Think it's the one that belched its way past your house on Sunday?"

"Looks similar. Can't say for sure."

"Did you get a look at the guy driving it?"

"Not really. Wasn't he wearing a big-ass hat of some kind?"

"Hell, I can't remember. I was focused on the brush across the street."

Mike picked up the latest cut-and-paste letter. "This has to be faxed to LAPD. He practically admits to being at the scene."

"Which makes him a murder suspect."

Mike inserted the letter in his fax machine and sent it on its way. "And he knows you're involved. How'd he do that?"

"Way I figure is he got the plate off my car. Looks like he traced it somehow to my name. He even showed up at my office this morning."

"We'll get him, Mr. Ford," Reggie said. "We've got a partial license plate."

"I hope so, Reggie. He's getting too close."

Chapter Twenty-Two

I sipped a cup of coffee and watched television coverage of helicopters bombarding the hills with water cannons. It didn't look as if they were doing any good. For the life of me I can't understand why people continue to build and buy houses up in those canyons, which, this time of year, become furnaces waiting for a spark. But then, considering my apartment is only big enough for me to change my mind, what do I know.

From the outer office I heard Mavis coming to work. I rinsed my coffee cup, shut the windows and tilted the floor fan toward the ceiling. Then I donned a hat and made my way to the front office.

"Morning," I called out.

"Hi, Eddie." Her voice came from her little alcove. "This faucet is still leaking. That clown better show up today."

I grabbed one of the 3 x 5 photos off her desk. "I'm going to swing by and pick up Reggie. Then get the printouts from Lieutenant Rivers. I'll drop Reggie off with them."

"How many names you think there'll be?"

"I don't know. Several hundred, I would imagine."

She flipped the switch for the ceiling fan, stood behind her desk and booted up the computer.

"So, what do your instincts tell you? You think Reggie's

going to work out?"

"Maybe. Some of that police academy learning might have rubbed off on him. Just be aware, though. He told me yesterday he's a little uncomfortable being around a lady."

"Oh, pish, I think we'll get along just fine. What's your agenda after you get the printouts?"

"Venice. See if I can talk to this Whit Baxter."

"Maybe he's the guy in the van."

"Now, that would simplify things, wouldn't it?"

I opened the door and looked back at her. "Go easy on the plumber."

"I won't make any promises."

I didn't see anyone who looked like a plumber on the way to my car. Too bad. The guy needed a heads-up.

***

Reggie was leaning over the second-story railing of his motel as I pulled into the lot. He bounced down the stairs, looking fresh and ready to go.

I pulled out into traffic and headed for LAPD's Hollywood Station. Reggie picked up the jewel case for the CD filling the car with fiddle music.

"The Skillet Lickers. Man, you got some funky tunes, Eddie."

"Plenty more in the back seat. You get some breakfast?"

"Yup, yup. Found a Starbucks."

Over dinner last night I'd gone over this whole case with Reggie. Told him what both Jack Boylston and Mickey Patterson had related to me concerning the events surrounding the *Red Desert* shoot. He'd listened attentively and asked pertinent questions, actions which made me think my Reggie experiment would prove to be right.

"Mavis said you don't have to worry about being nervous around her."

"Really?" He ran a hand through his hair. "Well, she's real nice."

"I think you'll get along just fine."

Hollywood Station sits across the street from Potter's Bail Bonds. Real estate agents always extol the virtue of location, location, location. If that's true, Mr. Potter's shop had to be a gold mine.

There was a parking space in front of the oblong brick building. I shut off the car and opened my door. "Let's go pick up those printouts."

Reggie sat staring at the front door. "Why don't I wait for you here?"

"Lieutenant Rivers is a good guy. Not to worry."

"'Member when I told you I'm a little gun-shy around women?"

"Yeah. So?"

"Same thing with the cops, Eddie. I'd be a little jumpy in there."

I looked at him and realized he was serious. "Suit yourself. I'll be back in a minute."

"Okay."

I got out of the car and walked to the front door. Reggie had told me he'd been picked up on a loitering charge. Could there be something in his background more serious? It was probably a good idea to have Charlie run a check.

A woman with skin the color of caramel sat behind the receptionist's desk. She had a head full of carefully cultivated corn rows and a name tag on her uniform blouse that said Evans. I told her I needed to speak to Lieutenant Rivers. She picked up a phone and said Charlie would be right with me.

On the walls were pictures of fallen cops. I glanced at a few of them and was struck with how young they had been. I heard a door open behind me and Charlie came through, a manila envelope in one hand, a folder in the other. He wore a short-sleeved white shirt, perspiration half moons under his arms. His necktie was askew. He looked uncomfortable.

"How you doin', Charlie? Staying cool?"

"As long as I'm in here." He handed me the envelope. "Here you go."

"How many hits?"

"I was told seven hundred and thirty-two. He then opened the folder and held up a fax. "Got this from Mike Ford yesterday. Why is your name on it?"

"He hired me to see if I could find out who's been sending him those letters."

"Running that partial plate have anything to do with it?"

"Matter of fact it does, Charlie." I showed him one of the pictures Mavis had printed out. "This was taken outside Ford's house yesterday morning. The guy was delivering phone books. That's his van."

"Who took this?"

"A guy I've got working for me."

He looked at the photo for a long moment. "Can you leave this with me?"

"It's the only one I've got with me. I'll have my secretary send you copies."

"Do that. But in the meantime." He handed the photo to the receptionist. "Fran, copy this for me, will you? Enlarge it if you can?"

"Sure thing." She took the photo and put it into a copy machine behind her.

"I'll have my people run another search," he said. "If we've got the vehicle, there should be fewer hits."

"The guy mentions the Ebersole woman in the letter. That could mean you've got a murder suspect, right?"

"Possible. You and Ford know each other?"

"For years. We came out here about the same time."

"Has he seen that picture?"

"Yeah. He doesn't recognize the guy."

"How about the van?"

"Not really. It might have driven by his house on Sunday morning when I was over there. We're not sure."

He took the photocopy of the picture from his receptionist. "Keep me in the loop on this thing. Hear me?"

"Will do." He gave me the photo and put his copy back in the folder with the fax.

"I got one more little favor, Charlie."

"What now?"

"That guy I said I've got working for me? Name's Reggie Benson. He told me he got picked up on a loitering charge. I might want to get him his license down the road. Can you stick him in the system and see if he's got anything more serious against him?"

Charlie pulled a notebook from his shirt pocket and wrote the name down. "What's his address?"

"Right now he's in a motel. Just got into town a little bit ago."

"I'll see if anything jumps out and give you a call. Also if we get a shorter list on that partial plate."

"Thanks."

I gave him my cell number, we shook hands and I thanked the receptionist as I walked through the front door.

Reggie was leaning against the car and hopped back in as I came out. I handed him the envelope. "Little over seven hundred hits. I showed Rivers a picture of the guy and the van. He's going to run another check. The list could wind up being shorter."

"In the meantime we should start on this one, right?"

"Exactly. Have Mavis make a list."

"Gotcha."

The Skillet Lickers finished fiddling and I put the disc back in its case. "So, you all right with doing this stuff with me and Mavis?"

He looked out the front window for a long moment. "Yeah, I just hope I don't screw things up for you, Eddie."

"How you going to do that?"

He shrugged. "Well, I been doin' that a lot the last few years."

I punched him on the shoulder and said, "A new

beginning, right?"

He turned to me, a huge grin on his face. It looked good on him.

Chapter Twenty-Three

Whit Baxter lived in an apartment building that resembled a long motel stretched along one side of Mildred Avenue. Come to think of it, that was probably its function back in the days when tourists hopped on Pacific Electric Railway's Red Cars and came to frolic at Abbot Kinney's seaside resort.

Metal screen doors on the apartments were flanked by single windows, facing the south and all the sun. But here in Venice I don't suppose heat ever became much of an issue. The building was pale yellow in color. At the center a switchback staircase led to the second floor. I walked up the steps to the address Mavis had given me and knocked on the screen door. It was slightly warped and rattled when I hit it.

Down below me an elderly Hispanic woman walked along the street, her hands full of bulging plastic bags. I rapped on the door again. The adjacent apartment opened and a young woman came out, pushing a bicycle in front of her. She had sandals on her feet, wore shorts and a loose tie-dyed tee shirt. Thick sunglasses covered her eyes and a floppy hat was on her head.

"Good morning," she said. "You looking for Jimmy?"

"Whit Baxter, actually."

She leaned her bicycle against the railing and locked her door. "Oh, that's his stage name. We all know him as

Jimmy Whitmore. He had to change it."

"Ah, that's right, I forgot," I said, suddenly remembering what Jack Boylston had told me. "These actors, you know. Never sure who you're talking to."

She pushed her bike in front of me on the way to the stairs. "Yeah, a little problem with that James Whitmore guy from *The Shawshank Redemption*. You ever see that?"

"Sure did. Whitmore did a pretty good Harry Truman too." I think I caught her by surprise because she turned and looked at me. I pulled one of the photos from my shirt pocket. "Have you seen Jimmy around this morning?"

"I did earlier. You want me to give him a message?"

"That's okay. I'll try and catch up with him later." I handed her the photo. "You ever see this man visiting him?" I was hoping that she'd tell me the guy next to the beat-up van was Jimmy Whitmore, aka Whit Baxter. No such luck. She looked at the picture and shook her head.

"Doesn't look familiar to me. Has Jimmy done anything wrong? You a cop or something?"

"No, no, nothing like that. I had a little fender bender with that van, and now I can't find the driver. Jimmy was a witness. Thought maybe he knew the guy and where he lives."

She pushed the bike toward the steps. I reached out and grabbed it by the seat and the handlebars. "Here, let me give you a hand with that." I picked the bicycle up and carried it down the stairs.

"Thanks," she said, as she came down the steps. She perched on the bike's seat and looked at me. "Harry Truman, huh? I'll have to check it out."

"Yeah, you should. *Give 'Em Hell, Harry*! is the name of the movie."

"Okay. Have a nice day." She pushed off, headed toward Venice Boulevard.

I turned around and walked in the direction of the sand. Whit, Jimmy—whatever the hell his name was—needed another visit. I was at the end of the block when my cell phone went off. I fumbled for a moment or two and finally pulled it from my pocket.

"Eddie, it's Charlie Rivers."

"What's up?"

"I ran the name Reggie Benson. No hits. Looks like your guy's clean."

"Glad to hear it."

"When we re-run that plate, you want me to fax it to you?"

"That'd be great." I gave him the number. "Thanks, Charlie."

"You got it."

I pulled my notebook out of my pocket. "Give me your email and I'll have Mavis shoot copies of those photos to you." He gave me the address and rang off. I called Mavis, gave it to her and asked if there was any progress with the possible plate matches.

"A little, but it's slow going."

"I can imagine. Lieutenant Rivers should be faxing you a shorter list soon."

"Great." She dropped her voice. "Eddie, Reggie is pretty sharp. He catches on right away."

"Glad to hear it, kiddo."

I closed the phone and slid it back into my pocket. Charlie had indeed provided good news. Given the fact that Reggie had been living on the streets, I could understand his discomfort around cops. Hopefully that feeling would recede with a roof over his head and the possibility of a steady paycheck.

My car was in a parking lot off Pacific Avenue. As I neared it, I glanced across the street and saw Jack Boylston standing at an intersection, swatting his leg with a battered baseball cap. He was looking in all directions like he was lost. Finally he started walking east. I dodged traffic, crossed the street and stuck my head around the corner.

"Hey, Jack."

He turned when he heard his name being called and slapped the cap back on his head. "Collins?"

"It's me."

"Christ almighty, I see you more than I do my proctologist. You live out here?"

"No, I was trying to talk to your friend Jimmy."

"Yeah, well, good luck with that. He ain't there."

"So I see. Where you headed?"

"The old lady's probably ready to send out a posse. I better get my ass home."

"Well, you're going the wrong way. Come on, I'll walk with you."

I guided him back to the corner. We waited for the light to change and walked north on Pacific. Venice was already bustling with people, some seeking relief from the heat, others filling out the cast of denizens that defines this peculiar neighborhood.

"What you want from Jimmy?"

"I need to ask him some questions about Mike Ford."

"You ain't gonna get much help there."

"Why not?"

"Jimmy don't think much of him."

A young kid on a skateboard barreled toward us. I pulled Jack to the curb and he flew past.

"Watch where you're goin', asshole!" Jack yelled. The skateboarder raised his middle finger in reply. "Goddamn kids. Hope he wraps himself around a telephone pole."

"Why doesn't Jimmy like Mike Ford, Jack?"

"You're gonna have to ask him."

"It have anything to do with him serving some time up in Barstow?"

Jack stopped and whirled to face me. "How'd you know about that?"

"Ford told me. Jimmy was convicted on a rape charge, right? You remember when it happened?"

"Some of it. You're talkin' a while back." We came to the end of the block and he looked up at the street sign. "This is it, right?"

I nodded and pointed down the street. Jack edged to his right to catch a sliver of shade from the buildings. I pulled out the photo of the yellow pages deliveryman and handed it to him.

"Does this guy look familiar?"

Jack held the picture at arm's length. "Who the hell's he?"

"That's what I'm trying to find out. Ring a bell with

you?"

He kept tromboning his arm and finally said, "Oh hell, I need my glasses. Can't see the nose in front of my face."

We continued on down the street. Jack had a little hitch in his step and almost stumbled over a bulge in the sidewalk from some tree roots. I grabbed his elbow.

"You all right?"

He got his balance and said, "Yeah. City outta dig up them damn roots."

"Jimmy ever talk about what happened up there in Barstow?"

He turned to look at me. "You're bound and determined to keep digging up shit, ain't ya?"

"I'm just trying to find out who's behind these letters Ford's getting. If somebody's got a grudge."

"Yeah, well, you can count me in on that one."

"So, did you send them?"

He abruptly stopped and grabbed my arm. "You're blowin' smoke up my ass here, Collins. I don't even know where the goddamn guy lives! How the hell am I gonna send him letters? If I wanted to settle a grudge, I'd do more than play post office with him." He waved his hand in dismissal and continued walking.

"You remember a kid by the name of Mickey Patterson that worked on *Red Desert?*"

He thought for a minute. "Yeah, I think so. Little smart-ass. He's on some show now." He pulled a handkerchief from his pocket and blew his nose. "He rape somebody too?"

"He said rumors were floating around the location

that maybe Jimmy didn't do it."

Jack put his handkerchief back in his pocket and adjusted his cap. He stared down at the ground. "Yeah, I heard about that."

"You think it's true?"

"Aw, Christ, I don't know. Even the goddamn Marines got involved. You'd a thought there was a rebellion or something."

We came to the front gate of the Boylston house. "You maybe better ask hot-shot director Ford what the hell happened."

"What's that supposed to mean?"

"He was running the goddamn show. Seems to me he'd have the answers." He opened the gate and turned back to me. "You still want me to look at that picture?" After I nodded he said, "Well, come on in then. I can use you as an excuse to the wife." We walked onto the porch. The front door was open. Through the screen Helen saw us and came scurrying up.

"Jack, where in the world have you been?"

"Over to Jimmy's." He pulled the screen open and we walked in. "Collins here ambushed me." He flipped his cap in the direction of a hat rack but missed the mark and the cap fell to the floor.

Helen picked it up and flicked a piece of lint off the crown. "Mr. Collins, did you find him lost again?"

Jack snorted and began muttering as he walked into the dining room.

"No, he was fine, Helen. I just wanted to ask him a few questions is all."

We walked into the dining room to see Jack pawing through the drawers of a sideboard. "Jack, why did you have to go to Jimmy's?"

"I had to get the key back." He found a pair of reading glasses, perched them on his nose and gestured for me to give him the picture.

"What key?"

"To the Kagel Canyon house."

"Why in the world would Jimmy have that key?"

He took the picture from me and peered at it, holding it up to the light coming through a window. "He said he'd go up there and check on the place. With all the fires and stuff."

Confusion washed over Helen's face as she walked into the kitchen. Jack looked at the photo, took off his glasses and handed it back to me.

"I don't know who this guy is."

"You sure?"

"Hell yes, I'm sure. I forget a thing or two, but never a face."

Helen came back from the kitchen holding a ring with a single key on it. "The key to the house is right here, Jack."

Surprise washed over his face as he said, "Well, I'll be damned. When did he bring that back?"

"Are you sure you even gave it to him?"

"Yes, I'm sure, for cryin' out loud." He tossed his glasses back into the drawer and started for the back room. "Am I gonna see you again tomorrow, Collins? We can maybe make up a bed for you."

I put the photo back in my pocket. "No need, Jack. Thanks for your help." He waved his hand and disappeared into the rear of the house. I gave Helen's arm a squeeze and she followed me as I started for the front door.

"I swear, I don't know what he's talking about, Mr. Collins. The next-door neighbor up there kind of looks out for the place and lets us know if anything's amiss. My goodness, I don't even know this Jimmy Whitmore very well. I don't know why Jack would trust him and give him the key."

"Well, maybe he just thought he'd given it to Whitmore."

She stood looking at the floor, running the key ring through her fingers. "I suppose." I opened the front door and stepped onto the porch. "Thank you again, Mr. Collins."

"You're welcome, Helen. Take care of yourselves." I doffed my hat and she responded with a wistful smile and a small wave of her hand.

Chapter Twenty-Four

As I walked back to Pacific Avenue, my mind buzzed with what Jack Boylston had told me. Mickey Patterson had alluded to the same thing, the possibility that Jimmy Whitmore, aka Whit Baxter, had gotten a bum rap up in Barstow all those years ago, that someone else had committed the rape. If so, Whitmore's motive for wanting to get back at Ford loomed large. Since Mike was the director, it seemed natural for Jimmy to want to get even with someone in charge of the shoot. On the other hand, Mike had told me the production bailed Whitmore out. Unless Ford's production company made the picture, or Mike himself had a producer credit, Whitmore's grudge would seem to be misplaced. But why, after all this time, was someone trying to get even? The movie was a few years back. Why now?

My stomach started growling as I neared my car. I passed a convenience store and bought a microwavable cheeseburger. A scarred-up picnic table sat outside the door so I plopped myself down and proceeded to eat lunch. After a couple of bites I realized my mistake. Either their microwave didn't work or the LA Kings were missing a hockey puck. I washed down the taste with a can of beer, deposited the rest of the insult into a trash bin and walked back toward Mildred Avenue. A scruffy young kid approached, his appearance making me glad I was upwind.

"Hey, man, I'm tryin' to get something to eat. Help me out?"

I reached in my pocket, separated a dollar bill from my money clip and gestured to the store behind me. "If you're going in there, forget about the cheeseburgers."

"I will, man. Thanks." He shuffled off in the direction of the store, my food critique probably sending him in search of a liquid lunch.

***

Mildred Avenue was a very narrow street, made even more so now by a U-Haul truck taking up most of the thoroughfare. A young guy and a gal were in the process of pushing a mattress up the aluminum ramp protruding from the rear of the truck. Curses flew from both ends.

The midday sun was warm, considering the close proximity of the ocean. I climbed the switchback stairs again and knocked on Jimmy Whitmore's warped screen door. I was just raising my hand for a second attempt when the door opened.

The glare of the sunlight allowed me only to see a guy that looked to be just shy of six foot, thin, long brown hair framing his face.

"Help you?" he said.

I detected the odor of smoke, which came from a cigarette clenched between two fingers of his left hand resting on the doorjamb.

"Are you Jimmy Whitmore, also known as Whit Baxter?"

"Yeah. Who're you?"

"I'm a friend of Jack Boylston's. I believe you worked with him on a picture called *Red Desert* a few years back?"

At the mention of the film, he paused and took a hit off his cigarette. "What about it?"

"I'd like to ask you a few questions about Mike Ford. He directed the picture, right?"

He stepped up to the screen. His face was weathered, a moustache and soul patch surrounding his mouth.

"Who the hell are you, mister?"

I fished out my license and stuck it up in front of his face. "Eddie Collins. I'm a private investigator."

"What do you want with me?"

"Mind if I come in? Little warm out here."

After a moment and another puff off his cancer stick, he pushed the screen door open and stepped back.

It took me a couple of seconds for my eyes to adjust. When they did, I saw an apartment that indeed at one time could have been a motel room. An archway at two o'clock revealed a bathroom door ajar, the light on above the sink. An entertainment console containing a TV occupied space on the wall to my right. A small kitchenette, not unlike my own, filled the far wall. A small table and two chairs were placed about a yard from the sink and stove. To my left sat a sofa, which no doubt folded out into a bed. Magazines, newspapers and an empty pizza box were strewn across the top of a coffee table that had seen better days. A can of Red Bull perched on a corner. The room smelled musty, and was laced with the faint trace of marijuana.

"What's this all about?" Whitmore said, pointing me to

one end of the sofa.

He wore jeans and a tee shirt with a pocket that held his cigarettes. His arms were thin, veins protruding along the length of them. A tattoo of a heart with a dagger piercing it occupied most of his right forearm.

He pulled a chair up and sat at the other side of the coffee table. His right leg bounced slightly. Either he was nervous or the caffeine from the Red Bull made him jumpy. He extinguished his cigarette in an ashtray made to look like a miniature truck tire. A Zippo lighter sat next to it. I pushed aside a copy of the *Times* and sat down.

"Ford's been getting some threatening letters. I'm trying to find out who's behind them."

"I don't know nothing about any letters."

"I understand you did some time up in Barstow after the picture wrapped. For rape?"

The question caught him by surprise and he cocked his head as he stared at me. His voice dropped almost to a whisper. "How the fuck'd you find out about that? Boylston tell you?"

"No, Mike Ford."

He let loose with a derisive laugh and upended the can of Red Bull. "He also tell you who really did it?"

"You're saying it wasn't you?"

"I'm saying I got set up."

"By who?"

"Why don't you ask Ford?"

He took the pack of cigarettes out of his shirt pocket, stuck one in his mouth and lit it with the Zippo. His left leg now started to slightly bounce up and down.

"Are you saying Ford had something to do with it?"

He exhaled a cloud of smoke in my direction and leaned forward in his chair. His long hair fell over his face and he brushed it back over his ears.

"Look...what the hell's your name again?"

"Eddie Collins."

"Look, Collins, both the Marines and the production company of that fucking movie were looking for a scapegoat. The jarheads had to keep their noses clean, and the *Red Desert* front office looked the other way. That Mexican chick had hinges on her heels, man. She was high on something. Yeah, I balled her, but it was consensual. And I wasn't the only one."

"What happened?"

He took another hit off his cigarette, got up and pulled another can from his mini-fridge. He popped the top and sat down again, still perched on the edge of his chair. He pushed another strand of hair away from his eye.

"I took her back into the bar and a couple of Marines started hitting on her. They'd worked as extras. They were sitting at a table with Ford and some of the front office types. When I tried to help the chick, the fuckin' Marines pushed me out the door and roughed me up. I went back to my motel. The next thing I knew, the cops were knocking on my door. She said I raped her. Then they hauled my ass to jail."

"And the movie company posted bail, right?"

"Yeah, big fuckin' deal. So I could finish the shoot. When they wrapped, I was left on my own. No attorney, no testimony, nothing."

"So one can assume you've got a grudge against Mike Ford."

"You can assume whatever you goddamn please. All I know is I spent eighteen months behind bars for something I didn't do."

"Did you threaten Mike Ford?"

"Fuck no! I've never seen the asshole since then. I don't wanna see him. Far as I'm concerned, he doesn't exist."

I watched him as he snuffed out his cigarette and took another long pull off his can of energy drink. I'd obviously hit a sore spot with him. Understandable. If it was me in his shoes, I'd have one big-ass industrial resentment. I glanced around the room. Despite the presence of newspapers and magazines, I couldn't detect any evidence of them being cut up and pasted into cryptic letters. I pulled Reggie's picture of the van from my shirt pocket and handed it across the table to Whitmore.

"Ever seen this guy?"

He took the photo, leaned back in his chair and tilted the picture to catch the light coming in from a window over the kitchenette's sink. Suddenly his legs quit bouncing and he stared intently at the picture. After a moment, he again leaned forward and handed the photo back to me.

"I don't know who the hell that is."

He stuck another cigarette in his mouth and flicked the Zippo. It didn't catch. He flipped it shut, turned it upside down and pounded it on his knee. It caught on the second try and he inhaled deeply.

"Ever seen the van?"

"Nope."

"Can you think of anyone else on that shoot who'd have it in for Mike Ford?"

He picked up his drink and lifted it halfway to his mouth. "Look, Collins, I haven't seen Ford since then, I don't even know where the fuck he lives, and I'd just as soon not even talk about the son of a bitch."

He gulped another mouthful of Red Bull and slammed the can down on the coffee table. He glared at me through another cloud of exhaled smoke. I stood and took a card from my wallet. "Give me a call if you think of anything else, will you? My cell's on the back."

He took the card and got up as I started toward the door. "How's the career going? Getting any work?"

"Nah, shit, what career? With a record?"

I stopped in the doorway and looked back at him, his right elbow cradled in his other hand. "Well, good luck. Thanks for your time."

"Yeah, whatever," he said as he slid the door shut.

I waited for my eyes to adjust to the sun and walked down the stairs. I'd hit a trifecta. Patterson, Boylston and now Whitmore had all alluded to the possibility of the wrong person being convicted for rape. Who did that leave? Had Mike Ford not leveled with me?

As I headed toward the ocean and my parked car, I thought back to Whitmore looking at the photo Reggie had taken in front of Ford's house. One of the attributes I've developed over my years as an actor is the ability to read body language. I think I've become pretty good at it. From his reaction, I was certain Jimmy Whitmore knew the identity of the guy delivering yellow pages to Mike Ford's house.

Chapter Twenty-Five

"Hal, he's got a picture of you. Next to the van."

"So he's got a picture. Jesus, Jimmy, I don't have a record. He doesn't know who I am."

"But they can trace the plates."

"The plates are stolen."

"You never told me that."

"Well, I'm telling you now. From an SUV out in Riverside. And I removed the VIN number, so keep your shirt on, for God's sake."

Over the phone Hal could hear the click of a cigarette lighter and a quick inhale. He hadn't told Jimmy about Eddie Collins, and for the last five minutes he'd been getting an earful.

"Jimmy, listen to me. Don't worry about Collins. I'll take care of him."

"What does that mean?"

"Just what I said. He's my problem."

A deep sigh came from the other end of the line. "He spooked the shit out of me, Hal. He knew about my jail time. The guy had a picture of you. What's next? He starts following me?"

"Not unless you gave him reason to. What did you tell him?"

"Not a damn thing. I said he'd better talk to Ford." Hal heard another puff on the cigarette. "Maybe we better put this deal on the back burner."

Hal took the receiver from his ear and shook his head. Here he goes again. He upended the bottle of water in front of him.

"All right, listen. The kid's back in school. We'll do it tomorrow."

"You don't want to hold off?"

"No. If Ford's gone to the cops, we have to move."

"And Collins?"

"He's taken care of, Jimmy. He won't be a factor. Be here with your Jeep at six-thirty. You follow me to Pasadena."

"Okay, but man, I am one nervous dude."

"I understand. We're good. I'll see in the morning."

Hal broke the connection and stared at Ford's Oscar sitting on the corner of his coffee table. He'd about had it with his so-called partner. The constant second-guessing, complaining. But there wasn't much he could do about it. Jimmy had the leverage with Ford they needed. The visit with the Mexican woman insured that. She was ready to talk if they asked her to.

He drained a plastic bottle of water in front of him, crushed it and threw it in the trash. He opened the closet door and rummaged around one of the shelves. There it was. His jump rope. With the wooden handles.

He sat at the table, picked up the scissors and cut the rope next to each handle, then pulled the ends through. He measured a piece of the rope fifteen inches wide, cut it and threaded both ends back through the handles. He tied a double knot on each end of the rope and yanked on it.

The knots held. It should do the trick. The element of surprise would be essential.

Chapter Twenty-Six

Julio Menendez should have been a demolition derby driver. As I watched him whip cars around his Victory Parking lot, I wondered what his insurance premiums must be. He squeezed a Mercedes next to the eight-foot cyclone fence surrounding the lot and came shuffling up to me. He was short and wiry, unruly hair sticking out from under a beat-up Dodgers cap. He wore a tattered short-sleeved shirt and faded jeans.

"You got the perfect timing, Eddie. This lady keeps forgetting to pay me. I got to say *adios*." He pulled a notebook from his hip pocket. "What's your girl's name again, *amigo*?"

"Mavis."

He jotted the name down and pointed to the space he had just cleared. "That's her spot. Tell her to leave the keys in the ignition." He handed me a window sticker. "She needs to put this on the inside of the front window."

"You've got someone in here twenty-four seven?"

"I got two nephews who were in Desert Storm. They split the shifts."

"I need to make sure she's going to be safe."

"Nobody gonna fuck with them, *jefe*."

"She'll be here in the morning. Thanks, Julio."

"*Bienvenido*. She have any problems, let me know."

I nodded, climbed in my car and drove to my office.

The temperature difference between Venice and Hollywood got me thinking about moving again. I pushed the thoughts away and rode the relic of an elevator upstairs.

Mavis was hunched over computer printouts.

"Hey, boss man," she said. "How was Venice?"

"Cool. Temperature wise, that is." I handed her the parking tag. "You are now official. Stick this on your windshield and leave the key in the ignition."

"Great. Thanks, Eddie."

"Where's Reggie?"

His voice came from my office. "In here."

I stood in the doorway and saw him at my desk. "You running the place now?"

He stood up and pushed the chair back. "Sorry, I—"

"Oh, sit, sit. I'm just yankin' your chain." I tossed my hat over a hook on the door. "How goes it with the lists?"

"Pretty slow. But I got about thirty possibles."

I turned to Mavis. "And you?"

"Eighteen."

"Charlie said he'd run those numbers again. Narrowing it down to vans."

"That's what we're working on," Mavis said.

Reggie picked up his printouts, walked into the front office and sat in a chair in front of Mavis's desk. "There's something I'm wondering about, though."

"What?"

He picked up one of the photos of the van and handed it to me. "Look at that license plate."

I did. "Yeah, so."

"That van is a few years old, but those plates look new."

Mavis looked at another photo and said, "Maybe he got new ones."

"Could be," Reggie said. "But what if they're stolen?"

"Good point," I said.

We both stared at Reggie and Mavis finally leaned back in her chair and threw down her pen. "Crap. Which means we're wasting our time with these stupid printouts."

"Aw, Christ," I said. "Did you send those photos to Lieutenant Rivers."

"Yes."

I pulled out my cell phone and dialed Charlie's number.

"Rivers."

"Charlie, it's Eddie. Got a new wrinkle."

"What?"

"You get those photos of the guy and the van?"

"Right in front of me."

"The plates on that van look like they're new."

After a moment he said, "You're right." Another pause. "Are you thinking what I'm thinking?"

"That they might be stolen?"

"Yeah." I heard a deep sigh on the other end of the line. "We'll have to tap a different data base. I'll get back to you. Probably won't be until tomorrow."

"Talk to you then." I broke the connection and looked at my two printout people. "Sorry, guys. More data on its way."

Mavis began shutting down her computer. "It's not going to make any difference, Eddie. If the plates are stolen, there's no way we're going to find out who that

166

guy is."

"Not necessarily."

"What do you mean 'not necessarily?' Did the cops run the photo of him through the system?"

"I don't know. I assume they did."

"You assume? Didn't you ask?"

"I will when I talk to Rivers in the morning."

"In the meantime, we've been ruining our eyesight for nothing."

"Come on, Mavis, lighten up."

She locked her desk drawers, stomped into her pantry alcove and turned off the light. "Why didn't you think of this before we started?"

"Think of what?"

"That those plates might be stolen."

"It never occurred to me."

"It occurred to Reggie. And he doesn't have the PI license." She stared at me, hands on her hips.

She had me. I glared back. After a minute, she grabbed her purse from her desk and opened the door.

"I'll see you in the morning."

And she was gone, leaving silence in her wake. Finally, Reggie cleared his throat and stood up. "Sorry, Eddie, I didn't mean to create a fuss."

"Don't worry about it. You didn't." I picked up the photos and flipped through them.

"If the cops have a picture of this guy, they'll run it through their system, won't they?"

"That's my assumption." I tossed them back on the desk. "But if he's kept his nose clean, it's a moot point."

"Well, maybe he didn't."

"Yeah, maybe."

Reggie shifted his weight from one foot to the other like I'd seen him doing on the Santa Monica pier. After a moment he said, "I'm kinda tired, Eddie. I think I'll head out."

"I'll run you home."

"Aw, it's okay, the walk'll probably do me good."

"It's no problem." That's when I heard my stomach growl and realized it had been a while since I'd encountered the convenience store hockey puck.

"You hungry?"

He shrugged his shoulders. "Yeah, I guess I could eat."

I grabbed my hat. "Ribs sound good?"

"Wow. Been a while since I had any of them."

"Let's get the hell out of here."

***

There was a Tony Roma's on La Cienega that wasn't too packed. After we settled in, I ordered onion rings to start, followed by a beer and a slab. Reggie asked for a Coke and seemed a little tentative looking at the menu.

"Go for it," I said.

He did. I think he felt a little out of place. We sipped our drinks and watched a family of four in a booth across the aisle. Two young boys had barbecue sauce from head to toe. Mom was facing serious laundry.

"So what did that Jimmy guy say, Eddie?"

The waiter delivered the order of rings and we dug in. I told Reggie about my conversations with both Jack Boylston and Jimmy Whitmore.

"That don't sound good for Mr. Ford, does it?"

"No, it doesn't."

"You known him long?"

"We came out here about the same time. Fifteen, eighteen years ago."

"Think he's got any reason to hide something from you?"

"Not unless he committed the rape."

"You gonna talk to him tomorrow?"

I spread more ketchup on my plate and smeared an onion ring with it. "Don't see how I can avoid it."

"Yup, yup. Three guys now been hinting something else happened on that movie. If it was me, I'd want more answers."

The waiter came with our orders and I watched Reggie attack his ribs. Even though the guy had been on the streets for several years, I was struck with the instincts he had. He was right. There was more behind that *Red Desert* movie shoot than I'd been told. Mike Ford had more explaining to do.

Chapter Twenty-Seven

I dropped Reggie at his motel and headed back to the office. Johnny Cash kept me company with his old standard "Busted." Appropriate title. That's what Mavis had done. Busted me. Pulled my covers. I should have looked more closely at the photos of that van. I didn't have an answer as to why I hadn't, except for the fact that I'd been preoccupied by my old friend Mike Ford having fingers of suspicion pointed at him all day.

I nudged the car into my parking slot and got a nose full of smoke when I opened the door. To the northeast, evidence of the fires loomed over the hills. The elevator door creaked open and the smell was replaced by perfume. Lots of it. I immediately let fly with a sneeze that knocked my porkpie askew. One of the models from the Elite Talent Agency had obviously been in here. Probably more than one. If these girls thought they were impressing their agent, they'd better wear something other than Chanel No. 2.5.

As the door slid open on my floor I pulled a handkerchief from my hip pocket. I reached my office door and erupted again, this time convulsing like someone had hit me in the gut.

As I put the handkerchief to my nose, I sensed movement to my right. I wasn't quick enough. A cord whipped around my neck, digging into my right wrist and shoving the handkerchief against my mouth.

The cord tightened, crunching my hand into my face, choking off my air supply. I twisted my head and managed to suck in a breath of air. More pressure from the garrotte bit into my wrist, pushing it against my windpipe. Dizziness began to cloud my head. I groped behind me, hoping to find clothing, hair, anything. I found an ear and yanked. Whoever was behind me pulled loose, did a three-sixty and smashed me into the wall, dislodging a cheap landscape print from its mooring.

The painting crashed to the floor, shattering the glass. My foot encountered a shoe and I stomped. He grunted in pain and twisted the garrote tighter. My wind was being cut off. The dizziness increased, my legs started to feel like Jell-O. With my free hand I grabbed the cord and pulled. A little less pressure. Mustering all the strength I could, I lunged backwards, forcing the two of us across the corridor and into the other wall.

I bent forward and tried to throw the guy over my back. No luck. His weight made me collapse to the floor with him on top of me. He had the advantage and used it to pull the cord tighter. I was choking, black spots swimming in front of me. I made an effort to crawl out from under him, but the lack of oxygen prevented me from getting anywhere. I tried to roll over. His knees had me pinned. Then I tried bucking him off. Same result.

I kept trying to loosen the tension on the cord with my left hand. I couldn't get my fingers between the garrotte and the side of my neck. I started to lose consciousness and heard a voice shout "Hey!"

I felt the cord loosen and heard more yelling. Finally, it fell from my neck and his weight came off my back. I rolled over and saw a black-clad figure ducking into the stairwell. I grabbed a foot and the guy hit the deck. Before he could take off, I struggled to my feet, got him by the shoulder and spun him around. A ski mask covered his face. I drew back and punched him where I thought his nose would be. Pain shot up my arm. He lost his balance and staggered back. I latched onto the collar of his shirt and rammed him into the doorjamb. He grunted and doubled over. I dug my fingers into the mask and slammed his head into the metal fire door. He bounced back and stumbled toward the stairwell. I lurched after him, but my foot slipped on a piece of broken glass and I lost my balance. I rammed my shoulder into the doorjamb. When I righted myself and got to the head of the stairs, I heard footsteps pounding on the steps several flights below me.

I staggered back into the hall and fell to my hands and knees, gasping for breath. And smelling perfume. I looked up and saw a tall willowy brunette in the middle of the hallway. The figure was out of focus. She grabbed my arm as I started to keel over.

"Are you okay?"

I sucked in huge gulps of air, trying to focus on the pair of high heels that swam in front of me. I nodded and mumbled, "Yeah."

I straightened up and was finally able to focus on my right hand. The knuckles were bloody, as was my wrist. The cord had gouged a good-sized welt where a watch would be worn. Too bad mine was on the other arm.

"Thanks for spooking him," I said. "I'm Eddie Collins." I offered my right hand, thought better of it, and stuck out the left.

"I know. I've seen you coming and going. I'm Vikki Tyler."

I bent over to pick up my key ring and had to steady myself with a hand on the doorknob of my office.

"Do you want me to call 911?" she said.

"Thanks, Vikki, but I'll be all right." My assessment might have been doubtful, since it took all the strength I could muster to pull myself to my feet.

"You sure? It's no trouble."

"I appreciate it. But not to worry."

"Okay," she replied, and walked to the elevator.

"Oh, by the way," I said, "I like your perfume."

Chapter Twenty-Eight

Even with the windows open and the morning not half over, the inside of the van was sweltering. Hal knelt by the sliding door in the back, cracked just a tad so as to open quickly. His forehead had a bandage over one temple and discoloration revealed the onset of a black eye. He and Jimmy were parked underneath a tree, half a football field from the school. Hal watched his partner behind the wheel, cigarette going full-bore.

"Don't you think we've got enough smoke with all the fires, Jimmy? Put that damn thing out."

"Yeah, yeah." Jimmy snuffed out the butt in the ashtray, adjusted the latex glove on his hand and glanced over his shoulder. "You should have let me help you. Two of us would have taken care of Collins."

"How was I to know the bimbo was going to come out of that office? It was after hours."

"Yeah, well, now what are you going to do about him?"

"When we place the call to Ford, I'll tell him to bring Collins along."

"And then what?"

"I haven't got it figured out yet, Jimmy. Jesus! Lighten up, will you?"

Jimmy shook his head, reached for another cigarette, then thought better of it. "You gotta keep me in the loop more, Hal. I could have helped with Collins. And the plates. You shoulda told me you were going to switch mine too."

"Sorry. I thought I did."

"Don't know why that was necessary."

"For God's sake, Jimmy, it's pretty obvious. You've got a record. Your name is going to be in the system. Right?"

"You don't have to keep reminding me."

"We can't have your vehicle traced."

They'd switched the plates on Jimmy's Jeep before heading to Pasadena. He'd parked the vehicle around the corner from the school, after which Jimmy drove the van to the Pasadena house of Ford's wife, Hal riding shotgun. They'd parked across the street and waited. They needed to see how the girl was dressed. Trying not to be conspicuous, they'd put magnetic signs on both doors of the van denoting the name of a phony plumbing company.

The two men had watched as the woman put her daughter in a dark blue SUV. The little girl wore a white blouse over yellow pants. As the mother drove off they'd followed her back to the school. Now all they had to do was wait for recess.

Jimmy looked over his shoulder again. He pointed to a bottle of chloroform sitting in a cup holder attached to the back of the front seat.

"You sure you know how much of that stuff to use?"

"Don't worry. I researched it online."

Hal loosened the cap on the bottle and the odor filled the back of the van. A burst of voices drew the two men's attention to the school. The doors had opened and children began streaming onto the playground.

"Start it up," Hal said.

The van came to life. Jimmy spotted the girl. "There she is, running to that merry-go-round." The two men watched Ford's daughter push the ride to get it going and then hop on.

"Go, Jimmy."

He slammed the van in gear. Hal's latex-covered hand pulled a handkerchief from his shirt pocket and poured a small amount of the chloroform onto it. Jimmy screeched to a stop beside the curb. Hal slammed the sliding door open, jumped from the van, yanked open a gate in the wire fence and ran to the merry-go-round. He grabbed the girl around the waist. She screamed and grasped the iron railing. Hal clamped the handkerchief over her nose and she grabbed his wrist. He pulled her off the ride and ran toward the van. The girl's shoelace caught on a jagged piece of the wire fence. Hal pulled the shoe off, jumped inside and shouted, "Go, go, Jimmy!"

The van shot away from the curb and barreled down the street. Jimmy careened around the next left turn, skidded to a stop behind his Jeep and jumped from the van. He yanked open the Jeep's rear door and Hal piled in, the girl motionless in his arms. Jimmy slammed the door shut and jumped behind the wheel, fired up the vehicle and squealed off.

Chapter Twenty-Nine

The guy with the garrotte had left a pretty good welt. A hefty dose of hydrogen peroxide and ointment made my wrist and hand feel better, but they still hurt like hell. The remedies didn't help me sleep, though. Most of the night I'd tossed and turned. Then I'd paced, trying to erase the feeling of helplessness that came with being unable to breathe. I'd just finished wrapping the banged-up wrist in gauze and tape when I heard the office door open, followed by "Eddie?"

"Yeah, I'm back here."

"Why in the world is all that glass lying in the hallway?"

I pushed through the beaded curtain and entered my office. "The janitor is supposed to clean it up. Guess he hasn't gotten here yet."

She stuck her head through the door. "What the heck happened?" She saw my bandaged wrist. "Oh, my God, don't tell me you cut yourself? You were mad at me so you took it out on a painting?"

"Nothing so melodramatic, kiddo." I filled her in on the events of the previous evening.

"You think it was the creep who was up here before?"

"That'd be my guess."

"Let me see that bandage." She picked up my hand and gave it the once-over. "Well, it'll have to do. Does it hurt?"

"Only when I shoot pool."

She rolled her eyes and started back to her office. "I see another attempt on your life hasn't prevented you from being a smartass."

"Yeah, well, I should have called you in the middle of the night. You could have watched me being a basket-case."

"Couldn't sleep?"

"Not much."

She stopped and turned back to me. "Hey, listen, I'm sorry about jumping on you yesterday."

"No worries. I had it coming. I lost my focus."

"How so?"

"Three different people have hinted Mike might have had something to do with that rape out in Barstow. That's not the Mike Ford I know. It's been weighing on me."

"What does he say?"

"That's what I'm going to find out." I grabbed my porkpie off the hook. "I called Reggie. He said he'd walk over here. I don't know if it's going to do any good, but you might as well keep looking over those printouts. You okay with that?"

"No problem. He's nice to have around."

"Good. I'm off to Ford's office." I opened the door and turned back to her. "The parking space okay?"

"Perfect. Thanks for doing that."

"Catch you later," I said and went out the door. Alfred Morales, the janitor, was sweeping up glass.

"*Mi Dios,* Mr. Collins. What happened here?"

"Disgruntled client, Al."

"Maybe you better get a different line of work."

I pushed the elevator button and thought about what he'd said. I have a different line of work, Al. Or so my agent keeps telling me.

***

Jimmy turned onto Kagel Canyon and looked in the back seat. The girl was lying in Hal's lap, still out.

"Shouldn't she be awake by now?" he said.

"Pretty soon. She's breathing fine."

The Jeep climbed up the road, air conditioning pouring cool air into the vehicle. To their right over the crest of the hills the sky was filled with smoke. They came to the adobe home and turned left. Both men looked at the old woman's house as they drove by. No one outside. Jimmy parked the Jeep and helped Hal climb out. He opened the front door of the cabin and stepped back as Hal carried the girl inside.

While Jimmy cranked up the window air conditioners, Hal carried the girl into the bedroom where the toys were. He placed her on the bed and pushed a strand of hair away from her forehead.

When he came into the kitchen, Jimmy had popped open a bottle of water. "You want one?"

Hal nodded and took a chair at the table. Jimmy handed him the plastic bottle and sat across from him. "When you gonna call Ford?"

"Right now," Hal said. He pulled a cell phone from his pocket. "This is a burner. Can't be traced." He looked at a slip of paper with Ford's number and dialed. "Peek in on the kid, why don't you?"

Jimmy walked to the bedroom as Hal started speaking

into the phone.

***

Clara Jesperson stood at her kitchen sink washing her hands. They were just filthy. She didn't think her simple search for that little stepladder would result in her getting so dirty. There's another project, she thought, squaring that garage away. Have to take some of that junk to the Goodwill when it cools off. This heat took all the gumption out of her.

She shook the water from her hands and reached up to grab a towel off the hook. Her attention went to a car going into the driveway of the Boylston place. She didn't recognize the vehicle. Looked like some kind of Jeep.

She watched as one of those young men got out and went around the other side. Then she saw the other one carrying something in his arms. Why, it looks like a child. Funny. They said they were screenwriters. They didn't say anything about one of them having a child.

I should give Helen a call, she thought. Find out more about those young men. Better do it later. Dr. Phil is due to come on. Can't miss Dr. Phil.

Clara dried her hands and hung up the towel. She took a bottle of iced tea from the refrigerator. The diet citrus kind. Coming, Dr. Phil, coming.

Chapter Thirty

I'd called Ford's office earlier and was told he was on Stage One at Paramount, helping to work out some shooting problem. He was producing the film. They told me they'd leave my name at the gate and I should go to the stage.

At Windsor I turned off Melrose and drove through one of the two iconic Paramount arches. I parked in the lot and walked up to the gate. The guard checked off my name on a clipboard and asked me if I needed directions. I told him I didn't. Somewhere in the annals of the Collins career there was a sitcom I had filmed on this lot. As I walked to Stage One, I tried to recall what it was. The name eluded me. Obviously, it hadn't been a hit.

The red light above the door wasn't turning, indicating it was safe to enter. I let my eyes adjust and looked around the stage. It was a whir of activity. In the center of the cavernous room I saw Mike huddled in conversation with two men and a young woman.

I stepped over cables and dodged moving scenery as I made my way to the center of the room. I hovered nearby until I caught Mike's eye. He held up one finger and went back to his discussion.

Sitting in tall director's chairs nearby were two of the current Hollywood hunks-of-the-month. If memory served me correctly, neither one of them had struck box-office gold lately. Come to think of it, one of them had recently gotten into a scrape with some paparazzi. See my movies, but don't take my picture. A familiar mantra. Mike finished his conversation and walked up to me.

"Your office told me where to find you," I said.

He nodded his head in the direction of the door and we walked. "Any news?"

I told him of Reggie and Mavis's efforts with the computer printouts, and the potential stolen plate issue. "You sure you don't know the guy by the van?"

"I've got two interns going back through files on every movie. So far nothing."

We walked across a studio street and into the main office building. Parkwood Productions was up one flight. Mike checked messages in an in-box and led me into his office.

"Coffee?"

"Sure. Black."

I sat in front of his desk and he dropped down behind it, leaned forward on his elbows. As I raised my coffee, he noticed the bandage on my wrist.

"What the hell happened to you?"

"Your phone book deliverer jumped me last night outside my office. At least I think it was him. Tried to wrap a piece of rope around my neck."

"He got into your building?"

I nodded.

"How?"

"He must have picked the lock. That's all I can figure."

"Why's he after you? Thought I was the one he wants?"

"Maybe he thinks I know who he is."

"The cops run a check on him?"

"They couldn't find a match." I sipped some coffee and set the cup on a coaster. "I've got some questions, Mike."

"Shoot."

"Mickey Patterson, Jack Boylston and Jimmy Whitmore all say I need to talk to you about what really happened on that *Red Desert* shoot."

He leaned back in his chair and looked at me over the rim of his cup. "What do you mean?"

"Whitmore hinted that he may have been set up for that rape."

"By whom?"

"He's not sure, but he thinks you know something about it."

"He's crazy. The girl identified him."

"He says she may have been with someone else that night."

"Yeah, there were some Marines around."

"At the bar? When she came in with Whitmore?"

"Right."

"He says you were there as well."

"For a bit. I left shortly after."

"You're sure, Mike?"

He leaned forward in his chair. "What are you trying to say, Eddie? That I raped the girl?"

"No. I'm trying to determine if Whitmore's the one who's got this grudge against you. Tell me what happened."

He finished his coffee, walked to a sink in the corner of

the office and rinsed out the cup.

"I was there with my AD and some of the crew. We'd had a few pitchers of beer, winding down from the day."

"Was Jack Boylston there?"

He sat behind the desk. "I think he was. But I can't be sure."

"Go on."

"Whitmore came in with the girl and sat at a table. Some of the Marines started hitting on her. Nothing serious. Just flirting. I left and went back to my room. That's all I know. Later that night cops knocked on my door and I found out what happened."

"If the girl says Whitmore raped her, why would she come back into the bar with him?"

"Good question. I don't know."

Lois Moore, Mike's assistant, stuck her head in the door. "Phone call, Mike."

"Tell them I'll call them back."

"You better take this. It's Courtney's mother. She sounds upset."

Mike punched the blinking key on his phone and picked up. "What is it, Brenda?"

He listened and his brow furrowed. "When?" I could hear his ex's voice on the other end of the line. "I'm leaving now." He slammed the receiver down, stood and reached for his keys on the desk.

"What is it, Mike?"

"It's Courtney. Somebody's grabbed her."

Chapter Thirty-One

We squealed out of the Paramount lot and headed north on Wilton to Franklin. The car ahead of us suddenly decided to make a left turn halfway through an intersection. Mike pounded the steering wheel and laid on the horn.

"You want me to drive?"

"I'm all right."

The car made its left turn and we continued barreling up Wilton. The light caught us at Hollywood. Mike banged his forehead on the steering wheel. I heard a huge sigh.

"Dammit, I should have hired someone to look after her when all this crap started."

"You had no way of knowing this would happen."

"The guy stole a picture with Courtney in it."

"Not to blow my own horn, Mike, but I'm in the picture too. Maybe this asshole has got a grudge against the two of us. He paid me a visit, remember?"

"So what the hell does he want?"

"I don't know. But the cops are going to be all over it. We'll find out."

"If anything happens to—" His voice caught in his throat and he pinched the bridge of his nose. "If anything happens to that little girl, Eddie, I'll never forgive myself." The light changed and we took off. He veered into the right lane.

"Did Brenda give you any particulars?"

"No. She was hysterical."

We hung a right at Los Feliz and hooked up with the I-5 and then the Ventura heading east. The Rose Bowl flew past on our left as we hit the Foothill Freeway.

When we rounded a corner and came up on the school, Pasadena patrol cars were spread out and uniformed cops were interviewing teachers and neighbors. People stood on the curbs, gawking.

We spotted Brenda and started toward her but a uniformed cop stopped us. Mike identified himself to a plainclothes detective who walked up. I showed him my license and he looked at me like I was a leper. But he allowed us to proceed to where Brenda was talking to another detective, this one in shirtsleeves with his badge hanging from his breast pocket.

Ford's ex-wife was tall and blonde. Her sunglasses were propped up on her head and her arms were flailing. She saw us, whirled on Mike and got in his face. "How could something like this happen, Mike?"

"Brenda, listen—"

"No, you listen. My little girl has been kidnapped. Who could do something like this?"

"I don't know."

"Somebody in that Hollywood crowd of yours?"

"That's not fair, Brenda."

"My God, Mike! You told me a picture of her was stolen when your house was broken into. Some one in your crowd knew it was there. What am I supposed to think?"

"We'll get her back, Brenda. Calm down for a minute." He tried to take her in his arms, but she broke away from him.

"You go to hell!" She pushed him away and let a uniformed cop lead her to some shade under a tree.

The detective in shirtsleeves walked up. He was a sturdy black man with a shaved head and a no-nonsense aura. He offered his hand to Mike. "Detective Evans. You the girl's father?"

"Mike Ford." He shook the offered hand and gestured to me. "This is Eddie Collins. He's a private investigator I've retained."

I again showed my license and in return got a onceover upgrading me from leper to pariah.

Evans handed back my ticket and said, "What's your involvement, Mr. Collins?"

"The guy's been sending threatening letters. I was hired to see if I could find out who he is."

"And have you?"

"Not yet."

"I see." He held up a plastic evidence bag containing a small tennis shoe. "One of the teachers saw this get caught on the wire fence. The guy pulled it off, so we may be able to get some prints."

"Anybody get a good look at him?" Mike said.

"Only from a distance. Witnesses say there were two of them. They drove off in a brown van."

Mike and I exchanged glances as I pulled my notebook from my pocket. "Did you get a plate?" I asked.

"Not only that. We've got the vehicle. Unfortunately the VIN has been removed and the plates are stolen." He handed the evidence bag to a criminologist and said, "Walk with me, gentlemen."

Brenda was engulfed in tears as a female officer led her to the merry-go-round. She sat on the edge and we followed Evans down the street to the first intersection. We turned the corner and saw the beat-up brown van next to the curb, surrounded by yellow police tape.

"The kidnappers obviously switched vehicles," Evans said. He pointed to a stucco house. "We've got a witness who said they saw some kind of Jeep parked in front."

I looked at the plate on the van and then at the numbers in my notebook.

"Five out of seven, Mike. That's the same van." I pulled one of Reggie's photos from my pocket and handed it to Evans. "Mr. Ford and I saw this van outside his house. The guy next to it is probably your man."

"He's also responsible for the death of my girlfriend," Mike said.

"How do you know that?" Evans asked.

"He implicated himself in one of the letters," I said. "Lieutenant Rivers, Hollywood Division, can fill you in."

Evans jotted down the name, flipped his notebook closed and put it in his pocket. "Let's hope we can get some DNA off this van and some prints from the girl's shoe." He stood in front of Mike and leaned in to him. "We'll find your daughter, Mr. Ford."

Mike turned and started walking back to the school. It didn't look like he believed what Evans had just told him.

Chapter Thirty-Two

Mike brought Evans up to speed on the letters and Janice Ebersole's drowning. A small cluster of neighbors still stood across the street, watching Pasadena PD escort children into vehicles containing anxious parents.

A tall man with a buzz cut of gray hair, wearing a dark suit walked up to us. His eyes were covered with sunglasses. Evans told us he was FBI Special Agent Ackerman. Mike and I introduced ourselves and I again provided my license. Because of the sunglasses I couldn't tell where I stood on Ackerman's social register. Evans handed him the photo of the phone book deliverer and repeated the information he'd gotten from Mike and me.

Ackerman escorted us to where Brenda was seated. He extended his hand to her. "FBI Special Agent Ackerman, Mrs. Ford. I'm very sorry about your daughter."

"Thank you," Brenda said.

Ackerman showed her the picture Evans had given him. "Does this man look at all familiar to you?"

She looked at the photo and shook her head. "Is he the one?"

"Possibly," Evans replied. "What about that van? Have you seen it sitting outside your home? Driving around the neighborhood?"

"Not that I can recall." She looked at the photo again, then turned to Mike. "This is outside your house, isn't it?"

Mike nodded. "After he delivered another letter."

She handed the photo back to Ackerman and he said, "Mr. and Mrs. Ford, the Pasadena PD has asked the Bureau to step in. We'll do everything in our power to get your daughter back safely. We don't know what the kidnappers want, so we have to assume they're going to contact either one of you. Consequently, we'll want to place a tap on your phones. Ma'am, will that be a problem?"

"No," Brenda said. "I'll go and open the house."

"Excellent. An Agent Carlson will meet you there." Ackerman consulted his notebook and turned to Mike. "We have a Nottingham address for you, sir. Is that correct?"

"Yes."

"A crew headed by Agent Fogarty is on the way there."

"Fine," Mike replied.

"I assume you both have cell phones?" Brenda and Mike nodded. "Obviously we can't confiscate them. If the kidnappers should call on a cell, we'll have a harder time tracing it. You can help us by furnishing the agents the names of your providers. If they should call we can access your records and start finding a tower. Any problem with that?"

They both shook their heads.

"What about your individual workplaces? Mrs. Ford, is there a place of employment for you?"

Brenda handed Ackerman a card. "I'm a design consultant and I work from home."

Ackerman took the card and slipped it into a shirt

pocket. "Mr. Ford, I assume you've got an office somewhere in Hollywood?"

"On the Paramount lot," Mike said.

"I imagine there's some sort of switchboard or receptionist a caller has to go through?"

"I've got three people in my office, two secretaries and my assistant."

Ackerman thought for a moment and replied, "I doubt very seriously if the kidnapper would call there, but you might want to inform your office of the possibility."

"I'll call them on the way to my house," Mike said.

Ackerman nodded and turned to Evans. "Anything else for now, Detective?"

"Just that we'll have surveillance on your home, Mrs. Ford, and I assume Hollywood Division will also be involved with regard to yours, Mr. Ford."

Ackerman and Evans moved off and Brenda turned to me. "Hi, Eddie. I didn't mean to ignore you earlier. I was a bit upset."

"Understandable," I said. "Sorry this happened."

She nodded and started to walk toward her car. Mike called out to her.

"Brenda?" She stopped and Mike walked up to her. "I'm sorry," he said. After a moment she nodded, then reached out and squeezed his arm.

"I'm sorry to hear about Janice," she said. "Let's hope they find this guy."

Mike watched her walk away. He turned to me and we walked back to his SUV. We climbed in and waited a moment for the air conditioning to kick in. Up the street a police tow truck rounded the corner, the brown van suspended by the rear end.

"She blames me," Mike said. "Big time."

"You can't hold yourself completely responsible, Mike. This guy obviously knows his way around a computer. He could easily have found Brenda's address and followed her here."

"Tell that to her." He reached over and turned the air conditioning down. "But it goes deeper, Eddie. She's never been comfortable with my professional circles. I've taken Courtney to shoots in the past and she's raised holy hell."

"That still doesn't mean you let this happen."

"Maybe not. But I could have hired someone to look after Courtney. You, for instance."

"Well, the feds are going to be involved now. They'll throw everything they've got at him."

"I hope that's enough."

We pulled away from the school and headed back to Hollywood. I couldn't help but think Mike was wrong in beating up on himself, but then it wasn't my daughter who had been kidnapped.

Chapter Thirty-Three

Jack Boylston's hand hurt like hell. The run-in he'd had with his hammer had resulted in the thing being thrown across the back fence into the alley. Of course the garage door didn't get fixed, but he could give a damn. His hand was bandaged up and throbbing. He sat in front of his TV, watching an episode of *Wagon Train*. Not a bad little part he'd had on that one. Got punched out by Ward Bond.

The cordless phone sitting next to him rang. He picked it up and croaked into the receiver. "Yeah?"

"Jack, this is Clara Jesperson."

"Who?"

"Clara. Your neighbor. Up in Kagel Canyon."

"Oh. Yeah. What do you want?"

"Let me talk to Helen."

"Helen? I don't know if she's here. Just a minute." He put the phone down and hollered her name toward the front of the house. She responded from the backyard.

"I'm back here. What do you want?"

"You got a phone call."

"Be right there."

Jack picked up the phone again and put it to his ear. "Hold on. She's out in the back. Killing weeds, or flowers, or some damn thing."

Helen entered through the back door, picked up the phone and walked into the front of the house. Jack muttered to himself and turned up the volume on the TV.

After a brief conversation Helen came back into the room. She put the phone down, picked up the remote and muted the television set.

"What did that Whitmore kid want with the key, Jack?"

"What key? Who?"

"The key to the Kagel Canyon house. That Whitmore guy. Did you give him the key?"

"Yeah, I might of. Why?"

"Clara says there's two guys in that house and they've got a child with them."

"I didn't know Jimmy had a kid."

"They told her they were writers."

"Writers? Jimmy ain't no writer."

"I think we better go up there and see what's going on, Jack."

"Oh, hell, he ain't gonna trash the place, Helen. Besides, it's too damn hot up there."

Helen glared at him, tossed the remote into his lap, picked up the phone and began walking out of the room.

"I swear, Jack, sometimes you're impossible."

She sat at the dining room table for a long moment, staring at the phone in her hand. Finally she pulled open a drawer in the sideboard and pulled out her little telephone directory.

***

On the way back to Mike's house we both had a turn with our respective cell phones. Mike called his office and informed his assistant, Lois Moore, of what had happened. Then my phone rang. It was Charlie Rivers.

"Eddie, those plates on that van were in fact stolen."

"Yeah, I heard. The FBI talk to you yet?"

"No. Why should they?"

I filled him in on what had gone down at the Pasadena school and our conversation with Agent Ackerman.

"Where's Ford now?" Charlie said.

"We're on the way to his house."

"Meet you there," he said, and rang off.

"They've got his picture," Mike said. "Can't they ID him?"

"Rivers said they can't find him in the system. The Bureau may have more luck."

"And in the meantime, we do what? Wait?" We started into the big curve off the Ventura leading to the I-5 south. "I don't know if I can do that, Eddie."

I reached over and grabbed his shoulder. "They'll find her, Mike."

We crawled up Nottingham and turned the corner to see two vehicles sitting in front of Mike's house. He parked the SUV by the garage and we walked back to the front door. A short, stocky man with closely-cropped red hair climbed out of one of the vehicles and met us. Behind him stood two more agents with briefcases and short hair as well. Whoever had the barbering concession with the FBI was cleaning up.

The agent flipped open a badge. "Mr. Ford, I'm Nick Fogarty with the FBI. I understand you've already talked to Agent Ackerman?"

"Yes. This is an associate of mine, Eddie Collins."

Fogarty extended his hand to both of us. I was relieved

to see I was no longer on the social misfit list. Mike ushered Fogarty and his crew inside.

"Do you have just the one telephone line, Mr. Ford?"

"Yes."

Mike gave them the name of his phone company, his cell provider and both telephone numbers, then walked into the living room and pointed to the phone. Fogarty gestured to his men and they opened their briefcases and booted up computers. He reached into an inside suit pocket and pulled out a document. "I'll need your signature, Mr. Ford." Mike gestured to the dining room table and they walked across the hall.

The doorbell rang. I answered it and Charlie Rivers walked in. I pointed to the dining room. He displayed his shield to Fogarty and Mike, then said, "Mr. Ford, we're going to have a unit staked out here twenty-four seven."

"Good," Mike replied.

Rivers and Fogarty moved into the hallway and began discussing procedure while the technicians continued to work on the phone tap.

Everybody in the house froze when Mike's cell phone went off. He pulled it from his pocket and looked at the display.

"It's my office. I'll send it to message and call them later."

He poked a key and replaced the phone in his pocket. Then he turned to me and the look on his face told me the call wasn't from his office. We walked into the living room and listened as both Fogarty and Rivers outlined what was going to take place.

"Mr. Ford, do you have any questions for us?" Fogarty asked.

"I do. I've got overseas investors coming in this afternoon to discuss a project that's been in the works for some time. That message may be about them. Am I tethered to the house?"

Fogarty looked at his technicians for a moment and said, "It would be best for you to be here to answer the phone."

"They've flown in from Japan," Mike said. "Couldn't the call be forwarded?"

Another look to the technicians, who both nodded slightly. "You have call forwarding?"

"Yes."

"If you absolutely have to leave the house, I guess we could forward it to your cell."

"I know this sounds crazy as hell, under the circumstances. Me wanting to leave. But I'm the one he'll want to talk to, right?"

"Right."

"I'm the only one who's got access to the cell. If it rings and I'm not here, you're monitoring it, aren't you?"

Fogarty nodded. "You'll have to enable it before you leave. Is there someone who can stay in the house? My agents should remain."

"I'll call my housekeeper. Her name is Angela Diaz." He pulled out his cell again and called the woman. She said she was able to come over. Fogarty and Rivers continued with their strategy session and Mike leaned into me and whispered. "We need to talk." I nodded and

Mike walked into the living room.

"I'm going upstairs to deal with my office," he said.

Fogarty nodded and we walked up the stairs. When we were out of earshot I said, "Who was that on the phone?"

"I don't know," he replied. We walked into his office and he shut the door. He touched keys on the phone. After a pause a girl's faltering voice was heard.

"Daddy?"

Mike collapsed into a chair and let loose with an audible sob. The voice paused and we could hear crying, then it continued through the tears.

"Daddy, I want to come home." The girl's voice faltered and a man was heard.

"Ford? She's a little scared, but she's fine. For now. Here's what I want you to do. The fart, barf and itch boys have probably got your phones tapped by now, so I want you to go to Collins's office. I'll call in an hour with further instructions. And Ford? Think twice about sharing this message with anyone."

The call ended. Mike dropped the phone on the floor and buried his face in his hands. I sat across from him and after a moment he looked at me, tears welling up in his eyes.

"Was it Courtney?"

He nodded and brushed the tears off his cheeks.

"You better go down and tell Fogarty," I said.

"You heard him, Eddie."

"What did you expect him to say?"

"I can't do it. Not yet. I can't risk them hurting her."

"You're withholding evidence. Breaking the law."

He picked up his phone and pressed more keys. "Not if there's no message."

"What did you do?"

"I deleted it. We'll wait for him to call."

"For crissakes, Mike! Do you realize what you're getting yourself into?"

"Listen to me, Eddie. Courtney is the center of my world. I'll do anything to keep her safe. No one is going to deny me that."

"What if you're sitting inside a jail cell?"

"That's a chance I'll have to take." He got out of his chair and paced to the other side of the office. "Put yourself in my shoes. You remember when you found out about that daughter of yours?"

"Yeah," I replied. In the wake of my ex-wife being murdered some months back, I'd learned that we'd had a daughter. She'd given it up for adoption without telling me. "What's that got to do with this?"

"Do you think if...Kelly...that's her name, right?"

"Right."

"If Kelly was in your life, believe me, Eddie, you'd do the same damn thing. You can't tell me you wouldn't."

I had to agree with him. I didn't know if I'd ever see this little girl, but I couldn't deny the number of times I'd thought about her since I'd learned of her existence.

"Okay," I said. "Point taken. But I still think you're on thin ice."

He sat down in front of me. I stared at him and saw the fear in his eyes. He fought back more tears and said, "I'm scared, Eddie. She sounded terrified. We've got to do what they say."

Common sense told me he was wrong, but I'd never seen him this shook up. "All right," I said. "How do you want to play it?"

"We can't leave together. Fogarty will know something's up."

"I'll ask Rivers to take me to my car. Those Japanese investors for real?"

"No."

"Well, tell Fogarty they have to see you. Go to my office. I'll meet you there."

Mike splashed cold water on his face and we walked downstairs. Lieutenant Rivers was shaking hands with the FBI agents.

"Charlie, you headed back to the station?"

"Yeah."

"My car's in the lot at Paramount. Can I catch a lift?"

"Let's go." Mike and I exchanged glances and I followed Charlie out the front door. He conferred with his stakeout team and we crawled into his car. He slid his windows down and we let the air conditioning kick in.

"Goddamn heat," he said. "I think my teeth are sweating."

"My socks are wet."

"*Touché.*" He rolled the windows up and we glided down Nottingham to Franklin. "Any idea who that guy in the picture is?"

"Has to be somebody Ford has run into in the business," I said. "I think something happened on that *Red Desert* shoot up in Barstow. But I'll be damned if I can figure out what."

As we dropped down Wilton to Melrose, Charlie filled me in on what they'd been able to find. It wasn't much. The plates on the brown van were stolen off a Lexus SUV out in Riverside ten days ago. He told me the phone book delivery guy still hadn't shown up in the law enforcement system. What I didn't tell Charlie is that he'd made his appearance on Mike Ford's cell phone. I had a burning urge to tell Charlie what we'd heard, but Mike was my client and if that's what he wanted to do I was willing to go along, albeit reluctantly.

Charlie dropped me at my car. I reached in and started it, then rolled down the windows and waited for cool air to circulate. Beside me, a guy fired up his motorcycle. I figured hot air was better than noise and carbon monoxide, so I climbed in and shut the windows. I'd no sooner done that than my cell rang. It was Mavis.

"What's up, kiddo?"

"Helen Boylston called again."

"What now?"

"She didn't say. You're supposed to call her."

"For crying out loud, why does she think she has to call me the minute Jack walks out the door?"

"I tried to get her to tell me the problem, Eddie, but she just said to call her."

"Yeah, yeah, okay."

I told her that Mike would be meeting me at the office and gave her the information about the cell phone message he'd received. I debated whether or not I should wait with the call to Helen, but figured I might as well break another law and talk to her while I was driving to my office. I pulled out of the Paramount lot, fumbled with the damn phone for a minute, trying to locate the Boylston's number. Helen picked up after three rings.

"Oh, Mr. Collins, you're such a sweetheart. Thank you so much for calling me back."

"What's going on, Helen? Jack take off again?"

"No, no, he's here. But I think there's something wrong."

"What do you mean?"

"You remember I told you we have that house up in Kagel Canyon?"

"Right."

"Well, our neighbor called. There's two young men up there. Clara said they're writers. One of them is that Whitmore fellow Jack gave the key to."

"So what's the problem, Helen?"

"I'm not sure. But this morning Clara said they drove away in a brown van."

I pulled over to the curb in front of a Subway sandwich shop on Vine and put the car in park.

"Say again? A brown van?"

"That's what Clara said. But here's the thing. They came back in a Jeep."

I turned the air conditioning down a notch to make sure I heard her right. "But no van?"

"That's right. And Clara said something else seemed funny about them."

"What?"

"They had a child with them. Clara said it looked like

one of them was carrying a little girl."

I pulled out my notebook. "What's the address of your house up there, Helen?" I jotted it down as she gave it to me and hung up. Jimmy Whitmore with a key to a secluded house. Where a brown van had shown up. And now a little girl. Coincidence? Maybe. But I doubted it. I found Mike's cell phone number and punched it in.

"It's Eddie. Are you still at home."

"About to leave. What's up?"

"We might have caught a break."

Chapter Thirty-Four

Hal sat on the sofa, running a soft cloth over the barrel of his handgun as he watched television news reports. Fire fighting crews reported the Angeles Crest Highway north of La Crescenta was in danger of being shut down.

All at once he heard the girl scream from the bedroom. He dropped the gun and bounded down the hall. He pushed the door open and saw her cowering on the bed, her back up against the wall. Jimmy sat in front of her, trying to touch her.

Hal grabbed him by the arm and yanked him into the hall. "What the hell do you think you're doing?"

"Nothing, man, I was just trying to play with her."

"Then why the fuck is she crying?"

"Why do you think? She's scared shitless."

Hal pushed Jimmy into the living room. "You're not helping. Stay away from the kid. Let me deal with her."

"Yeah, right, whatever."

Jimmy stiff-armed the door to the patio, stomped out and lit a cigarette. Hal picked up a package of Oreos off the kitchen counter, pulled a juice box from the refrigerator and went back down the hallway to the bedroom.

He pushed the door open. The air conditioner was going full-blast. The girl lay on the bed, curled in a fetal position, sniffling. He pulled a chair to the side of the bed and sat down. The girl's eyes widened in fright and she scooted back toward the wall. One little fist was in front of her mouth, a knuckle between her teeth.

"You okay?" There was no response. "Are you cold?" After a moment she nodded. Hal set the juice and cookies on the bedside table and turned the window unit down a notch.

"Did that man scare you?" She nodded. "He didn't hurt you, did he?" She stared at him and finally shook her head. "I won't let him hurt you. Want some juice and cookies?" She again shook her head. He opened the package of Oreos and put the straw in the juice box. "I'll leave them here for you, okay? Maybe you'll want them later."

She stared at him and gnawed on a finger. "I want my mommy," she said, her voice quaking.

"I know. But your daddy's going to come for you real soon. Remember when you left that message for him on the phone?" She thought for a minute and finally nodded. "Well, I left him one too. You'll see him after a while."

She sniffled and stuck out a foot. "I lost my shoe."

"I see that."

He went to one of the cardboard boxes in the corner and pulled out a pair of flip-flops.

"Why don't you give me your tennis shoe and you can wear these until we get you another pair, okay?"

After a long moment, the girl reached down and took off her tennis shoe and handed it to him. He gave her the flip-flops.

"They won't work with my socks on."

"You want to take them off too? I'll keep them for you."

She pulled off the socks and handed them to him.

"Your name is Courtney, isn't it?"

"Yes."

"That's a real pretty name." Hal handed her the juice box and she reached out and took it. "How old are you, Courtney?" She put the straw in her mouth and just stared at him. He held up five fingers. "Are you this old?" She shook her head. He held up four. "This many fingers?" Again she shook her head. "How many fingers?"

She set the juice box next to her and held up six fingers.

"Six? Wow. You're a big girl for six fingers." She picked up the juice box and her eyes widened as she looked toward the door. Hal turned and saw Jimmy standing in the opening.

"Hal, I need to talk to you."

Hal put his chair by the wall and said, "Courtney, you can play with any of the toys in these boxes. I'll be back in a little while." He closed the door and followed Jimmy into the front room.

"She okay?"

"She's fine. What's up?"

Jimmy walked to one of the windows and said, "Look at that."

Hal pulled aside the curtain and saw the old woman next door in her front yard, binoculars to her eyes.

"She's been standing there for the last five minutes looking at us. She sure as hell ain't bird watching."

"Maybe she's looking at the fires."

"Yeah, maybe. But I doubt it. She was on a cell phone just a minute ago." The two men looked at Clara

Jesperson until she lowered the binoculars and went back into her house.

***

Clara finished pouring herself a glass of nice cold lemonade and shut the refrigerator door. It was too hot to stay outdoors for very long. Besides, she couldn't really see anything inside the house anyway. All the curtains were closed. Kept the heat out. But she did see one of the young men come outside to smoke a cigarette.

She took a long swallow of the cool drink and put her binoculars in their case. She started to put them on the shelf in the hall closet but decided against it. Maybe she should have a look now and then. Helen had sounded a little concerned when she talked to her on the phone. She started down the hall to put in a load of laundry when she heard a knock on the front door. She opened it to find one of the young men. She'd forgotten his name.

"Hi, Mrs.—. I'm sorry, but I'm drawing a blank."

"Jesperson. Clara Jesperson."

"That's right. Clara. I wonder if I could ask a huge favor of you."

"Why don't you come in? Land sakes, you'll fry out there." Clara pushed open the screen door and the young man came inside. "Silly me, but now I can't remember your name."

"Howard, ma'am."

"Oh, that's right. Can I get you some lemonade, Howard?"

"No thanks, Clara. I'm fine. I can't seem to get any cell phone reception. Do you have any problem?"

"No, I don't," she said, pulling the phone from her pocket. "Plenty of bars on mine."

"Well, that's funny," he said. "I wanted to make a call and Uncle Jack doesn't seem to have a phone in the house."

"I know. That's his foolishness, the old coot. When they come up here, they bring their phone along with them. Helen keeps trying to get him to buy another one, but of course he won't listen."

"Makes sense, I guess. Person can't use more than one at a time anyway, right?"

Clara laughed and said, "That's what he keeps telling Helen." She closed the door and pointed to a wall phone in the kitchen. "That dang thing there doesn't work, and the only other one I've got is in the bedroom." She handed him her cell phone. "Why don't you just use mine? They sure are handy contraptions, aren't they?

"Yes, indeed," he said. "Thanks, Clara."

"I'll put my laundry in and let you make your call."

She toddled off down the hall and Hal flipped open the phone. He pushed several keys until he found the list of recent calls made. There it was. Boylston. Placed only fifteen minutes ago. Two other calls to the number had been made earlier in the day.

Clara came back down the hallway. "Are you sure you two are cool enough over there? I saw you--."

She stopped when she saw Hal pointing a gun at her.

"What on earth are you doing?"

Hal gestured with the gun. "Into the living room. On the sofa."

"My God, why are you doing this, young man?"

"You've been spying on us, Clara. I don't like a snoop."

"I haven't been spying. I—"

Hal pushed her down on the sofa and picked up one of the small pillows. "Then why the binoculars and the calls to the Boylstons? I think you're just a snooping old busybody."

"No, no, I was just calling them about the fires. Don't hurt me, please."

Hal jammed the pillow over her face and put his knee onto her chest when she started to struggle. He pressed the gun into the pillow and fired. Small tufts of stuffing flew out of the pillow as the woman went limp. Hal waited a moment, then removed the pillow. The shot was clean, right through the forehead. He used the barrel of the gun to move a strand of gray hair away from the entry wound.

He tossed the pillow aside and rose from the sofa. He stuck the gun down his belt at the small of his back and picked up the cell phone. He opened it, removed the SIM card and laid the phone on the kitchen counter.

He paused at the front door, listened, then walked down the hallway and raised the lid on the clothes washer. The machine stopped. Hal walked to the front door, looked back at the old woman on the sofa and exited the house.

Chapter Thirty-Five

I'm constantly amazed and envious of the way Mavis handles a computer. She's been attempting to get me computer-savvy. So far her efforts have yielded mixed results. However, watching her print out maps of the Boylston's Kagel Canyon address filled me with renewed inspiration.

Mike and I pulled computer images from the printer. He'd told Agent Fogarty the phony Japanese investors requested his presence and that he'd have to go to his office. Apparently the agent hadn't been too keen on Mike leaving the house, but in the end he'd relented. It looked like the ruse had worked.

The maps revealed the small Boylston house facing east toward hillsides of thick brush and sparse trees. Across the paved lane there were no homes, but rather a deep gulley, the other side rising toward the crest of a ridge.

"If you're convinced we should do this, we'll have to park down by that adobe house and walk in behind," I said. "There's no cover in front."

Mike picked up a couple of the maps. "Maybe we'd be better off going up there at night, Eddie."

Reggie had been watching us from my office doorway. "Good point," he said. "Looks like you'll have to cross private property to get to the house."

"That's true," I said. "But let's stop and take a deep breath for a minute. We better not think about doing anything until we hear from this guy." I looked at my watch. "The hour's almost up. He should be calling."

Mavis sent another map to the printer and leaned back in her chair. "I don't want to rain on your parade here, guys, but don't you think it would be a good idea to get the police involved?"

"We've already been through this," I said, looking at Mike. Both Mavis and Reggie did the same.

After a moment he said, "I know I'm in the minority here, people. But the guy said no cops. He's already invaded my privacy and killed my—" He stopped, bit his lip and forced back tears. "I cannot risk any harm coming to my daughter. Sorry, but that's the way it has to be." He reached out, took a tissue from a box on the desk and swiped at the corners of his eyes. "But you're right, Eddie. Let's wait to hear from him."

After an uncomfortable moment of silence Mavis said, "Okay. If it was me I'd probably want to do the same thing." She handed the last map to me. "That's as many as I can get."

I spread them over the desk. We had a pretty good idea of the way the neighborhood was laid out. The challenge would be getting to the rear of the Boylston house undetected.

The phone rang, causing Mavis to jump. She looked at us. I pointed to the speakerphone button and nodded. She picked up. "Collins Investigations."

"You've got a real cute secretary, shamus." It was the

same voice that had been on the cell phone message. "I suppose I'm on a speakerphone. You there Collins?"

"I'm here. Who is this?"

"All in good time. Is Ford there?"

I looked at Mike and he said, "This is Ford. I want to talk to my daughter."

"She left you a message."

"You could have faked the voice. Put her on the phone."

There was a pause and we could hear rustling on the other end of the line. After a moment, the caller said, "Say hi to your daddy."

Finally Courtney's small voice could be heard. "Daddy?"

Mike leaned over the phone. "Courtney? It's me, honey. Are you all right?"

"Yes, I guess so, but I wanna come home."

"I know, honey, and you will real soon. Has anyone hurt you?"

"No, but I lost my shoe."

Mike straightened up and inhaled deeply. I could tell he was trying to control himself. The man's voice came back on the other end of the line, "Ford, your daughter is fine. And she'll remain so as long as you do what you're told."

"What do you want?" Mike said. "Money? Name it."

"We can talk money later. In the meantime I want you to take a drive up into Kagel Canyon."

The caller rattled off an address. I checked it against the one Helen Boylston had given me and nodded to Mike.

"Be here at four o'clock. No guns, no cops, no Feds.

The only person I want you to bring along is your PI buddy Collins. We didn't get a chance to talk outside his office. You listening, Collins?"

"I hear you. You know, the cops have got your picture."

"So I gather. But they don't know who I am or where I'm at, right?"

Neither Mike nor I responded.

"Right, Ford? Did you hear what I said?"

"I heard you."

"You don't want to know what will happen if these instructions aren't followed."

The caller broke the connection and the four of us looked at each other for a moment. Finally Mike sank into a chair. "Oh, Christ. So much for catching them by surprise."

"Whitmore has to be his accomplice," I said. "I showed him the picture of the guy delivering the phone books outside your house."

"So there's at least two of them," Mike said.

I shuffled the maps into a single pile. "I don't know how the hell we're going to be able to get the drop on them. I mean, if that's what you're still thinking of doing, Mike."

"I don't know either, Eddie. But dammit, we've got to do what they say."

After a moment Reggie sidled up to the front of Mavis's desk. "You guys have an ace in the hole, Eddie."

"What?"

"Me. These guys don't know who I am."

Chapter Thirty-Six

Kagel Canyon Road meanders north off the Foothill Freeway near Lake View Terrace, the notorious locale where the late Rodney King had an unfortunate run-in with law enforcement. The aftermath turned the city on its head; sometimes I wonder if it's ever recovered.

Mike drove, I rode shotgun and Reggie was in the back of the SUV wearing a hard hat and a lanyard draped around his neck. After he'd suggested he was our ace in the hole, he'd come up with a possible means of getting to the rear of the Boylston house.

"Gimme a clipboard," he'd said. "Remember in the Army? If you had a clipboard under your arm you could walk all day. Everybody thought you were workin' on something."

I couldn't argue with the ruse. I'd done it myself a time or two. Reggie had embellished on his idea by having me find him a hard hat in my collection of audition costume pieces. I'd found a plastic lanyard and Mavis had come up with a phony ID photo. He was fully prepared to say he was scouting the neighborhood for possible fire hazards.

Given the way the skies looked to the east, he could very well be taken at his word. Helicopters flitted over the area, and off in the distance I noticed one of those water tankers let loose with an aerial bombardment. On the way up here we'd seen engine companies barreling eastward along the freeway.

I pointed to my right. "Is this guy going to think those are police helicopters?"

"They're too far off," Mike replied.

I turned back to Reggie. "You're sure you can do this?"

"Yup, yup, good to go." He flashed me a thumbs-up. "I'll try to get to the back door. If there is one."

"We don't know what these guys are going to do, Reggie," Mike said. "You'll have to play it by ear."

"Yup, I know. They're probably armed, right? If I hear shots, I'm comin' in." Mike had also supplied Reggie with a handgun, which he'd stowed in a pocket of the cargo pants he was wearing.

We continued to crawl up the narrow roadway. There was virtually no activity. The heat was probably driving everyone indoors. The houses were small and the entire neighborhood gave the impression of middle or lower-class squalor. There didn't seem to be a decent lawn anywhere. Here and there sat broken-down vehicles, dry brown weeds obscuring the wheels. A boat was perched on a trailer next to a double-wide.

Ahead of us on the right we spotted the adobe-looking house with a cedar fence around the perimeter of the lot. Mike pulled over and pointed to his left. "There's the road. See the water tank?"

"Right," I said. Reggie opened the back door and slid out. "Be careful."

"You too. Good luck, you guys. We'll get her back, Mr. Ford."

He nodded and we watched Reggie cross the road and

disappear into a small stand of pine trees. Mike put the SUV in gear and we crept up to the narrow lane and turned left. I looked at one of the maps in my lap and then at the small water tank off to our right, sitting on a patch of gravel.

We drove up the lane and off to our left saw a green Jeep sitting in the driveway of a small house with a patio to the right of the front door.

"That's it," I said.

Mike pulled in behind the Jeep, cracked the windows and shut the engine off. There was no sound except for gusts of wind that kicked up small whirls of dust and sighed through the pine tree above us.

"Do you see Reggie?" I asked.

"No."

We stared at the door and after a moment it opened. Out stepped the person Reggie had captured on film in front of Mike's house. He was bare-headed now, his hair cropped close. His forehead sported a bandage and I could see the beginning of a black eye. He had to have been the guy with the garrotte who jumped me outside my office. He wore jeans and a tan short-sleeved shirt, buttons undone, layered over a white tee shirt. He was thin, his face angular and filled with creases. His right hand gripped a serious looking semi-automatic. He glanced at the watch on his left wrist.

"Right on time. Get out of the vehicle. Slowly."

Mike and I opened our doors and slid into the heat. As I walked around to the other side of the SUV I pointed to the choppers flitting around the hills to the east. "Those aren't police."

"I hope you're right," he said.

"You got a name?" Mike asked.

"Hal Morrison. Ring a bell?"

Mike looked at me and I shook my head.

"Should it?"

"Yeah, but I didn't figure it would." Morrison glanced over his shoulder and called out, "Jimmy."

The door opened again and a second man stepped through the entry. It was the same guy I'd talked to down in Venice, Jimmy Whitmore. He shut the door behind him and stood next to his partner.

"Let's put the hands on top of the heads," Morrison said.

Mike and I complied. Morrison gestured with the barrel of the handgun and Whitmore walked toward us. He patted me down and looked Mike in the face before he started on him.

"Hey, Ford. Remember me?"

"I do. You were in *Red Desert*."

"Right. The guy you left in jail."

Whitmore finished frisking Mike and straightened up.

"Is that what this is about?" Mike asked. "Why you guys kidnapped my daughter?"

"Let's get out of this fuckin' heat," Morrison said. "Inside."

He motioned for us to enter the house. Whitmore got behind us. I hadn't seen evidence of him having a gun, but that didn't mean he wasn't armed as well. Mike and I walked to the front door, opened the screen and started to go inside. As I crossed in front of Morrison I gestured to the bandage on his forehead.

"What happened to your head? You run into a door?"

We did dueling glares as I stepped into the house. It was cool inside. An air conditioning unit groaned in one of the windows. I glanced down a hallway to the rear of the house. I could see a back door with a window in the center and through it a backyard. Reggie would be in luck. I hoped the damn thing wasn't locked.

Morrison shoved us toward the couch and Mike said, "Where's my daughter?"

"Take a seat and we'll talk about how this is going to go," Morrison said. We sat down. Morrison and Whitmore pulled up kitchen chairs and straddled them.

"She's back in one of the bedrooms," Morrison said. "I'm going to go get her. You two can have your touchy little reunion, then I want you to tell her to go back to the bedroom while you and I have business to discuss. Got it?"

"Got it."

Morrison handed the gun to Whitmore. "Don't let the kid see this." He got off his chair and walked down the hallway. Whitmore nervously bounced one foot as he held the gun on us.

I pointed to the jerky movement. "Nervous, Jimmy?"

"Nah. You're the one should be nervous, Collins."

"I didn't leave you in jail," Mike said. "There was nothing I could have done."

"Bullshit. You could have come forward with the truth." The foot stopped bouncing and he started waving the gun around. As nervous as he looked, I was expecting it to go off any second. He suddenly put the gun by his side as he saw Morrison come back down the hall.

Courtney shyly moved in front of him. When she saw Mike she cried out. "Daddy! Daddy!" She ran into Mike's outstretched arms. He wrapped them around her and she buried her face in his neck.

"Are you okay, baby? Did they hurt you?" She uttered a muffled reply and gripped Mike's neck. He rocked the girl in his arms as he watched Morrison lean on the empty kitchen chair.

After a moment or two she relaxed her grip on Mike's neck. He held her out in front of him and looked into her face. "Are you sure you're okay, honey?" Courtney nodded and self-consciously bit one of her knuckles. "We're going to take you home." He wiped the trace of a tear from one of her cheeks. "I have to talk to these two men for a few minutes, and then we'll go see Mommy, okay?"

She nodded again and pointed to her feet. "I lost one of my shoes."

"I see that," Mike said.

She pointed to Morrison. "He gave me some flip-flops."

"We'll buy you new shoes when we get home, honey. Can you go back to your room for a little bit while I talk to these men?"

She threw her arms around his neck. "I want to stay with you."

"I know you do, Courtney. But I'm going to be right here. We'll go in a few minutes, okay?"

Courtney looked at her dad for a long moment, nodded and then glanced over at me. A look of recognition crossed her face and she waved her little fingers. I returned her greeting and Mike kissed her and turned her around to face Morrison. He took the girl by the hand and led her back down the hall.

Mike buried his face in his hands, then looked to Whitmore, who had now lifted the gun and was pointing it at us again. "Have either one of you touched her?"

"We ain't harmed her, Ford. Quit worrying."

Morrison returned from the back of the house, reclaimed the handgun and again straddled the chair in front of us. Mike scooted to the edge of the couch.

"All right, what do you guys want? How much?"

"Shut up." Morrison almost shouted the command. I saw his jaw clench and he leveled the gun at Mike. "Think back to that movie up in Barstow you directed. *Red Desert.* My partner here did some time after you movie people left. Time he shouldn't have done."

My suspicions had been right. Both Jack Boylston and Mickey Patterson had alluded to something strange happening on that shoot.

"That's what he keeps saying," I said. "What the hell does that have to do with Mike?"

He looked at both of us for a minute. "Ford, does the name Rosa Moreno mean anything to you?" Mike thought for a moment and shook his head.

"Just what I figured," Morrison said, as he turned to Whitmore. "Jimmy, the floor is yours."

Chapter Thirty-Seven

Reggie wasn't used to this heat. He'd been on the streets in Santa Monica close to the ocean for a lot of months. It wasn't hot there like up in this canyon. He tucked the clipboard under his arm and walked up a makeshift alley between houses. The path was basically a set of parallel tire tracks, with a hump between them covered by oil-stained brown grass.

Aside from the wind the only sounds he heard were the thwacks of the helicopter rotors to the east. He noticed movement to his left and saw a dog bounding toward him, its leash tethered to a metal clothesline. The dog was a mutt, but seemed friendly. Reggie didn't see much shade for the animal. The poor thing was probably suffering. Stupid pet owners. The dog stopped, gave a little bark and sat on his haunches as Reggie continued on.

He spotted the Boylston's house to the right. Ford's SUV was in the driveway beside a Jeep. He was in luck. The house had a rear door with a window. As he started toward it, he heard the roar of an engine behind him. A firefighting unit churned up to the adobe house, pulled over and parked. The engine idled for a moment, then stopped and a helmeted firefighter crawled out of the cab and began speaking into a radio. To the southeast flames and thick smoke were visible on one of the ridges.

Reggie saw an electrical meter on the wall next to the rear door. He walked up, peered at the meter and made a phony notation on his clipboard. He looked behind him and grabbed the handle of the screen door. It opened and he slid his hand through the opening and slowly turned the knob. The door was unlocked. Good. He withdrew his hand and gently pushed the screen door closed.

He peeked through the window in the door. He couldn't see anyone. From a doorway on the right a man walked out holding the hand of a little girl. Reggie ducked back and wiped the sweat from his forehead. All right, she's okay. So far, so good. He'd have to wait. For what, he wasn't sure. He checked to make sure the pocket of his cargo pants was sealed. He ducked under the window and slid around the corner to the north side of the house where there was shade. He took off his hard hat, wiped his brow and sunk to his haunches with his back to the wall. Nothing to do now but wait. And listen.

***

I watched Whitmore take a crinkled envelope from his shirt pocket. He pulled out what looked to be a letter, unfolded it and held it up for Mike and me to see.

"I got this a few weeks ago. It's from Rosa Moreno up in Barstow. She worked on the movie, Ford. Bussing tables, doing clean-up for the caterer." He tucked the envelope back in his pocket and proceeded to read.

"'This is a very hard letter for me to write *senor*. But I have been bothered by my conscience ever since it happened. So a few months ago I talked to my priest. I confessed to him. I told him that I lied about who raped me when the movie was in town. I was forced to tell the police it was you, Mr. Whitmore. But it wasn't.'"

Whitmore flipped the page over and paused. I glanced over at Mike and saw an expression I'd never seen before. If what the woman had written was true, the suspicions Jack Boylston and Mickey Patterson had shared with me were also true. Mike would have a lot of explaining to do, not only to me, but everyone he knew.

Whitmore cleared his throat and continued. "'After we were together, I went back to that bar. The soldiers bought me some wine. The director of the movie... His name is Mike Ford, yes? When I left to go home, he followed me. I told him to leave me alone, but he forced me into an alley and then he raped me.'"

Mike erupted. "That's a goddamn lie! How do I know that letter is real, Whitmore? You've concocted this whole thing. What the hell do you want from me?"

He jumped to his feet and lunged for Whitmore. I grabbed him by the elbow and tried to pull him back, but not before Morrison leapt from his chair and cracked Mike on the side of the head with a large glass ashtray sitting on the coffee table.

"Sit down, Ford! Right now."

Mike collapsed on the couch. He put his hand to his left temple. Blood seeped through his fingers. He pressed a handkerchief to his head and glared at Morrison.

"You're going to regret that, pal."

"Yeah, right. Next time you'll take a bullet." Morrison hurled the ashtray into a corner, righted his chair and sat back down. Then he turned to Whitmore and said, "Go ahead, Jimmy."

Whitmore's leg started bouncing again. "I ain't makin' this up, Ford. She put her phone number in the letter. So I called her. Everything she said is the truth. She'll swear to it. Listen to this." He again referred to the letter. "'I don't know what I can do now, but I would be willing to tell the authorities if somehow you wanted to clear your name or something. I apologize for what I said back then. I hope you can forgive me.'"

Whitmore folded the letter and returned it to the envelope. He leaned back in his chair.

"So, what about it, Ford? You think maybe you owe me?"

"Owe you for what?"

"The time I spent behind bars, man."

Mike leaned forward, his hands on his knees. "Listen, you clown. This is ridiculous. You were convicted. You did the time. And now you expect me or anyone else to believe some trumped-up phony rape charge? Give me my daughter and let's be done with this crap."

Whitmore pulled a pack of cigarettes from his pocket, flipped one out, then thought better of it and put them back. He glanced over at Morrison, stymied, a look on his face asking for help.

"You're missing the point here, Ford," Morrison said. "Think about it for a minute. This woman comes forward, gets herself all lawyered-up. Hires Gloria Allred, for instance. Christ, man, you know how much that woman likes a microphone. Your career is going into the tank. Hell, I'll have to return your Oscar so you'll have some company."

The room fell silent, save for the groan of the air conditioning unit. Morrison had a point. I looked at Mike. I think he knew it too. His standing in the industry was at stake if there was anything to this letter. I wasn't about to admit that, but there was something I didn't understand.

"What's your stake in this, Morrison?" I said. "Sounds like you're putting Jimmy up to this. You weren't on the picture. You didn't do time. What do you want?"

Morrison leaned forward in his chair. His eyes turned cold as he pointed the gun at Mike.

"You, Ford. I want you. Dead."

Chapter Thirty-Eight

This could be trouble. When Reggie had heard the second engine company rumble up Kagel Canyon, he'd ducked under the rear window of the Boylston back door and peered around the corner of the house. To the southeast the flames and smoke had intensified. The wind had picked up. More firefighters climbed out of the second truck and talked on radios. Finally a red command SUV pulled up. More discussion, and one of the firefighters pointed to the surrounding homes. Another one walked up to the front door of the adobe house. Reggie could see a woman talking to the firefighter.

They were preparing the neighborhood for evacuation. The kidnappers weren't going to appreciate that. Reggie looked down the south wall of the house. Two window air conditioners protruded, both whirring at high speed. Eddie and Mike probably couldn't hear anything going on outside. Nor could the kidnappers. They wouldn't expect somebody banging on the front door. Should he create a diversion at the rear of the house? Pound on the door? Reggie decided it was too risky. No telling what these guys would do. Better to just wait and see what happened.

He went back to the north side of the house in the shade. There were two windows. The furthest contained another air conditioning unit. He crept down the side of the house until he came to the first window. A shade covered the opening, giving him nothing to see inside. The second window yielded the same result. He went back to the rear of the house, looked around the corner to see a firefighter striding toward one of the homes further south. It wouldn't be long before they'd be coming to the Boylston house. He was in plain sight. How would he explain his presence? He sank down on his haunches and wiped his forehead. Wait, just wait. But for how long?

***

Mike and I stared at Morrison. The room was silent, save for the steady drone of the air conditioner.

"Are you crazy?" Mike said.

Whitmore stood up, knocking his chair over. "Hal, no, wait, man, we never said anything about killing anyone."

"Sit down, Jimmy. You had your turn. Now it's mine."

"Come on, man, we said we were just going to blackmail him for work." Whitmore stepped toward Morrison. "This wasn't in the plan."

"Shut up, Jimmy!" Morrison jumped to his feet and stuck the gun in Whitmore's face. "Sit the fuck down or I'll shoot you first."

Whitmore froze, then finally picked up his chair and sank into it. After a moment, Morrison shifted the gun toward Mike and me. He showed none of the nervousness of his partner. The look on his face was piercing, determined.

"Hal, you better think this through," I said. "How do you know Ford hasn't got a GPS in his SUV?"

I was bluffing, of course. I hadn't noticed the device in Mike's vehicle, nor had he mentioned having one. But I hoped my ruse would buy us some time with this lunatic.

"Sooner or later they're going to trace the car."

"I thought about that, Collins. That's why this is going to happen sooner than later."

"What is this all about?" Mike said. "What the hell have I ever done to you?"

Morrison turned his chair so he was facing the two of us and perched on the edge of it, the gun still pointed in our direction.

"Flashback time, Ford. You weren't originally going to act in *Red Desert*, were you?"

Mike took the bloody handkerchief from his forehead. "No. My backers insisted I step in. They thought it would insure better box office."

"Do you know who was initially cast in that role?"

"I have no idea."

"You're looking at him."

Mike stopped fiddling with the handkerchief and looked up at Morrison.

"I'm sorry that happened, but it was out of my hands. If you had a deal memo, you still should have been paid."

"Well, you see, there's the problem. My agent called your office and got the brush-off. He was told the producers—meaning you, Ford—decided to 'go another way.' That lame-assed excuse you people always use when you've fucked over someone. When directors like you aren't happy enough picking up one salary, but have to take a job away from a struggling actor by sticking yourself in front of the camera."

He got up and began to pace in front of us. "What is it

with that anyway, Ford? Your ego's that big you can't stand to let someone else get a piece of the pie?"

"I told you it wasn't my decision."

"That's bullshit!" Morrison continued pacing, waving the gun in front of us. I didn't know if the damn thing had a safety, but as agitated as he was, I doubted he had it on. "What about you, Collins? You're an actor. You'd be pissed, wouldn't you?"

"It's happened to me many times," I said. "And yeah, it made me madder than hell. But it never caused me to start waving a gun in someone's face. Use your head, pal."

Morrison put one foot on the coffee table, leaned over and pressed the gun to my forehead. The metal was cold, like the look on his face. Shivers ran up the back of my neck. I'd never been this close to the business end of a firearm, and it scared the hell out of me. He bent over and looked me in the eye.

"Yeah, well, Ford here is your buddy, Collins. He would have taken care of you. Thrown you a bone."

He took the barrel of the gun off my forehead, backed up and sat on the edge of his chair.

"That little reunion you had with the girl was very touching, Ford. Reminded me of my daughter."

"Then why are you acting like a jerk?" Mike said. "Think of her because you're not going to get away this."

"I do think of her. Every day. Only one problem. She's dead. She died three months ago."

Morrison's words caught both Mike and me off guard. We glanced at each other and then at him. Finally Mike said, "I'm sorry to hear that."

"Pardon me all to hell if I don't believe you. You see, Ford, she was born with a heart defect. She needed an operation. Landing the *Red Desert* gig would have qualified me for the SAG health insurance. Instead, you took the job from me. I didn't have enough earnings and she couldn't get the operation. You have no idea what it's like to watch your daughter deteriorate in front of you. Without any means of helping her. The way I look at it, Ford, she died and you're responsible."

I said, "Hal, that's ridiculous. You can't blame your daughter's death on Mike. Killing him isn't going to bring her back."

"Oh, please, Collins, stop. My wife left and took the kid with her. That was before she divorced me and bled me dry with alimony. Her parents helped with the medical bills, but it wasn't enough. My daughter got steadily worse, and she finally died. So I'm not in the mood for your goddamn platitudes."

Whitmore's attention suddenly shifted to the window. He got out of his chair and pulled back the curtain.

"Hal, there's trucks down the street. Firemen are walking up here."

"Sit down, Jimmy. I'll handle it."

"You got your hands full. I better talk to them." He started toward the front door, but Morrison grabbed him by the arm.

"Lemme go, Hal. Keep an eye on the two guys you're so fuckin' intent on killing. I've had enough."

He shook off Morrison's hand and again moved toward the door. Morrison spun him around by the shoulder and jammed the barrel of the pistol next to his temple. Whitmore grabbed Morrison's wrist and pushed the gun away. The two men wrestled, each trying to gain control of the firearm. Morrison pushed Whitmore against a small bookshelf, but his feet slipped on the carpet and Whitmore managed to push him off. Morrison reeled backward, hit the floor and leveled the pistol at Whitmore.

The shot was deafening in the small room. Whitmore screamed, clutched his chest and staggered backward, knocking pictures off a television set.

Morrison rolled over on his left shoulder. I slapped Mike on the leg and whispered, "Now." He tossed aside his handkerchief and got to his feet, but I could tell he was woozy from the clout on his head. I upended the coffee table in front of me and lunged at Morrison. He got to one knee and fired another round. The shot caught Mike in the right thigh and he went down. I grabbed the hand with the gun and we wrestled ourselves into the kitchen, bouncing off the walls and crashing into the kitchen table.

Someone started pounding on the front door. I heard a voice shouting. From the altercation I'd had with Morrison outside my office, I knew he was strong. And he didn't disappoint. My bandaged right hand was failing me and I started to lose my grip on the hand with the gun. I stuck out a foot and swept his legs from underneath him. He lost his balance and fired another round. It plowed into the ceiling. He fell back and I lost my grip. I picked up a kitchen chair, hoping I could disarm him with it. The pounding on the front door started again and Morrison turned and fired into it. Then he righted himself and careened down the hallway.

I started to follow him, but crouched when he fired another round. The shot went wide. He ducked into a bedroom and I flung open the front door and saw a firefighter standing there.

"What the hell's going on? Someone shooting in there?"

"Yeah. Have you got a radio?"

The firefighter lifted his transmitter. "Right here."

"Get on it and send an ambulance up here. Two men are down. One with a chest wound."

He keyed his transmitter and I turned and hit the floor again as I saw Morrison burst out of the bedroom, the gun pointed at me. He had Courtney clutched under one arm. She screamed and kicked. He fired again and started for the back door of the house.

I could only hope he'd be met by Reggie.

Chapter Thirty-Nine

Reggie didn't know what to do. He stood at the southwest corner of the Boylston house and watched the wall of flame and smoke creeping up the gulley across the street. More trucks and firefighters had arrived. One of them strode toward the front door of the house. Whatever was going on in there with Eddie and Mike Ford was about to be interrupted.

All at once he heard gunshots from inside the house. He saw the firefighter crouch and then begin running toward the front.

Behind him the rear door banged open. A man carrying a girl under one arm burst out. She was screaming and kicking. Reggie recognized the guy as being the one he took the picture of outside Ford's house. He had a pistol in his right hand. Reggie hugged the wall and the kidnapper ducked around the north side of the house. He threw his clipboard to the ground, pulled his gun out of the pocket of his cargo pants and followed. When he rounded the corner to the north side the man was running toward the front of the house. Reggie aimed, but knew he couldn't risk taking a shot because of the girl. He began running after the kidnapper.

***

I leaned over Mike and handed him the bloodied handkerchief he'd been using on his forehead. Next to me the firefighter was crouched over Whitmore, talking into his radio. He'd ripped Jimmy's shirttail and was pressing the cloth against his chest wound.

"Keep pressure on that puncture, Mike," I said. Paramedics are on the way."

"I heard Courtney. Where's Morrison?"

"He grabbed her and went out the back. Don't worry. Reggie's out there."

"I stashed a gun under the front seat of the SUV if you need it." He gripped the front of my shirt, desperation filling his eyes. "Get her, Eddie."

"We will. You stay here." I crouched next to the firefighter and pointed to Whitmore. "He gonna make it?"

"The bullet went through. He should be all right. EMTs and cops are on the way. I'll stay with him."

I clapped him on the shoulder and shoved the front screen door open. To my left Morrison was running, Courtney still clutched under his arm.

"Morrison, let the girl go!" I yelled.

He stopped, saw me and pointed the gun. I dived behind the wall of the patio and the shot plowed into the two-by-four railing, sending slivers of wood into my hair. I looked behind me. Two more firefighters had been running up to the house. They'd hit the dirt when they heard the shot.

I peered over the patio wall. Morrison yanked open the front door of the Jeep parked next to Ford's vehicle. He cursed as he looked for the car keys. He slammed the door shut and repeated the search with Mike's SUV. He looked behind the visor and in the glove compartment.

Fortunately he didn't think to stick his hand under the seat.

Reggie appeared on the other side of the patio. He had his gun raised. He saw me and said, "That's the guy who delivered the phone books, right?"

"Yeah. His name's Hal Morrison."

"We gotta separate him from the girl, Eddie."

I nodded and watched Morrison as he slammed the SUV's door shut. He started toward the front door of the house but spotted Reggie and realized he was flanked on both sides. But Reggie had the gun, I didn't.

He fired another shot at Reggie and missed. I didn't know how many rounds his clip held. Getting shot at wasn't conducive to keeping track. Morrison stopped, retreated between the two vehicles and looked to the south where the fire was moving and firefighters were assembling. He took off across the road toward the gulley.

I yanked open the front door of Mike's SUV and found the pistol under the driver's seat. Reggie came up to me and pointed at Morrison running toward the gulley.

"He's not going to outrun that fire."

"I know. We've got to get Courtney away from him." We crouched down and began following. "Morrison, stop! Give up the girl. She's not going to do you any good."

Morrison stopped, turned, and fired. We hit the ground. He swung the gun toward the oncoming firefighters and pulled the trigger. Nothing. He'd run out of ammo. He kept pulling the trigger, finally threw the gun away, turned and started running. His feet got twisted up. He tripped over a rock and fell, losing his grip on Courtney.

The little girl righted herself and took off in our direction. One of her flip-flops came off but she didn't stop. I ran to meet her and scooped her up in my arms. She grabbed me round the neck. She was sobbing, deep gasps.

"It's okay, honey. You're all right now," I said. "I'll take you back to your daddy." I turned to Reggie. "See if you can catch him. Try and take him alive if you can."

"Right," he said, and took off across the street toward the gulley. Morrison had already disappeared. Into the path of an oncoming wall of flames and smoke.

Chapter Forty

A firefighting rig lumbered up the street, headed for the Boylston house as I ran with Courtney in my arms. Embers filled the air and I could see some of them land on the roof. She sobbed uncontrollably, despite my murmuring in her ear, telling her she was going to be all right.

I elbowed the front door open. Mike raised himself from the sofa and tried to get to his feet. I set Courtney down. She ran to him and jumped into his outstretched arms.

"Daddy, Daddy."

"Oh, baby. It's okay, honey, you're safe now."

I righted the coffee table and sat on the end of it. "How's the leg?"

"Better now that I've got this armful."

He stroked Courtney's hair and her sobbing started to lessen. Strips of white cloth were wrapped around Mike's thigh. The firefighter tending to Whitmore had apparently found some dishtowels and ripped them up for a tourniquet and makeshift dressing.

"You better give me the keys to your SUV. Reggie and I need a way to get out of here." Mike pointed to his trouser pocket. I reached in and found the clump of keys. "I'll catch up with you later."

Something slammed against the side of the house and

shouts were heard. I knelt beside the firefighter tending to Whitmore and offered my hand. "I'm Eddie Collins. Thanks for your help."

"Frank Hughes," he said as he stuck out a soot-covered hand. "Your friend over there has lost some blood, but I think I finally got it stopped. Paramedics are on the way." He gestured to Whitmore. "This one needs a hospital pretty bad. Both of them do, actually. You get the shooter?"

"My partner's chasing him. But he's going to need help."

"We'll have to evacuate these two, and everybody else. You better find him quick."

"Right." I heard more shouting and footsteps on the roof. As I started to get to my feet, Whitmore reached out and grabbed my arm.

"Hal's got a gear loose, Collins." He tapped the letter in his breast pocket. "When I got this we were just going to use it to pressure Ford into giving us some work, man. He never said anything about murder."

"Yeah, well, the cops are going to have to sift through it all. You better hang on to that letter."

Mike yelled at me. "Eddie, forget about him. Morrison's the one behind this."

"Yeah, yeah, I'm going," I said. I got to my feet and headed for the door. Outside, the smoke and flames continued moving north. The heat had intensified. Two firefighters on the roof sprayed it with water. I ran toward where Morrison had disappeared. No sign of either Reggie or him.

***

As he started running, Reggie stuffed his gun in the pocket of his cargo pants. With Morrison now unarmed, he wouldn't need it. He glanced to his right and heard fire crews yelling at him to stop. He paid no attention and ran across the street to the lip of the gulley. Smoke engulfed it. He heard the popping of dry wood as the fire swallowed up the trees. A gust of wind swept aside some smoke and he spied Morrison at the bottom of the gulley.

"Morrison, get the hell back here!"

Morrison turned to look, then started crawling up the far edge of the gulley. Reggie lost sight of him and started to make his way down the slope. The ground was covered with leaves and pine needles. He slipped and his yellow hard hat fell off. He managed to grab a tree root to stop his slide. Nothing stopped the advancing fire. Reggie's lungs filled with smoke and sparks landed on his head.

As he struggled to get a foothold, he heard a scream from the other side of the gulley. Morrison had grabbed a boulder to help him climb. The rock had come loose and rolled down the slope, taking Morrison with it. The boulder came to rest on the bottom with Morrison pinned underneath.

Reggie regained his footing and began creeping down the side of the gulley. He wished he had a handkerchief to put over his mouth. The smoke made him cough. His eyes watered. The wall of flames loomed about fifty yards down the gulley, consuming everything in its path.

He reached the bottom and ran toward Morrison. The boulder had both his legs pinned. Reggie grabbed the rock and pushed. It wouldn't move. He looked around for a branch to use as a lever. Through the smoke he saw a tall pine tree go up in flames. The tree started to fall in the direction of the boulder. It crashed to the ground, sending sparks and embers over both Morrison and Reggie.

***

I ran to the lip of the gulley and saw nothing but smoke filling a dry creek bed. The gulch was full of fuel for the moving inferno, fanned by the high winds. A few feet down the slope I saw Reggie's hardhat.

"Reggie! Where are you?"

At the bottom of the creek bed a tall tree burst into flames and started to topple. A sudden gust of wind cleared some smoke and I saw Reggie at the bottom. He was crouched behind a boulder that had Morrison lying underneath. The burning tree crashed to the ground about six feet from the two men. Embers landed in the dry leaves and pine needles, setting off small fires.

"Reggie, you've gotta get out of there!"

"Morrison's trapped. We need to move this rock."

I started to creep down the slope, slipped and fell on my ass. A six-foot log broke my skid. It lay along a small ledge overlooking the creek bed. I hunched over and started coughing from the smoke. A burning chunk of wood landed at my feet and ignited the ground cover around it. I stomped it out and brushed cinders off my clothing. Another gust of wind kicked up more embers and I felt the heat creeping up the dry creek bed.

Below me Reggie found a tree branch and slipped one

end of it under the boulder. He pried. The branch snapped. Morrison screamed as burning chunks of wood fell on him.

"Come on, Reggie. Get up here."

"What about him?"

"It's too late. You're going to be toast if you don't get the hell out of there!"

Reggie hesitated, then ran to the slope beneath me. He started to climb, but slipped back when he couldn't find toe or hand holds in the slick ground cover. I looked behind me and saw a smoldering tree branch. I grabbed one end and burned the hell out of my hand. I grasped the other end and stepped on the charred end, breaking off a two-foot chunk.

I leaned over the rim of the ledge. Reggie was still trying to get toe and hand holds. He wasn't having any luck. Behind him the flames crackled and started to ignite the side of the gulley we were trying to climb. I extended the branch toward Reggie, but it was now too short.

"Go to your right. I think I can reach you there."

Reggie crawled to his right and I skidded down a dip in the ledge. This time I could reach him with the tree branch. He grabbed and I pulled. His feet slipped and almost yanked me off the ledge. He dug the toes of his boots into the side of the slope and began to inch himself upward.

Behind him another tree exploded into flame, large branches snapped off and fell over Morrison. I heard his screams over the whooshing sound of the fire, as if the creek bed had been doused with accelerant.

Reggie looked back and then resumed climbing, his eyes wide with fright. I pulled the branch, wood splinters digging into my hands. I backed up and finally Reggie crawled over the rim of the ledge. He lay panting, coughs causing him to convulse. I grabbed him under the arms.

"Come on, the slope flattens out up here."

We scrambled along the ledge, embers and sparks raining down on us. Morrison's screams followed us, then finally stopped. The incline leveled off and we headed up, slipping and crawling, madly grabbing at anything we could find to give us something to hang onto.

The smoke in front of us cleared and I saw blue sky. We bounded up out of the gulley and looked behind us. The wall of flame had consumed the creek bed where Morrison lay trapped under the boulder.

Both of us leaned over and coughed, retching into the parched grass. Behind us I heard the shouts of fire crews. Overhead a water tanker swooped down the path of the burning creek bed. I wiped the sweat off my face and handed Reggie the handkerchief.

"I didn't think I was gonna make it, Eddie. I owe you one."

I flashed back to a night long ago in a Korean village and a young MP with martial arts skills making mincemeat of a drunken GI.

"You don't owe me anything, Reggie."

Chapter Forty-One

The Kagel Canyon blaze was under control. Reggie and I discovered that fact as we sat in front of my television set watching the news. We had a pizza spread out in front of us, picking up the slices with bandaged hands. We looked like a couple of lepers.

"There ain't gonna be much left of Morrison," Reggie said.

"Yeah, well, I'm not going to lose any sleep over his loss."

"Yup, yup. Me too."

After we'd crawled out of the burning gulley, we limped back to the Boylston house and saw two gurneys being lifted into ambulances. Ford and Whitmore. Firefighters sprayed the roof of the house next door. We piled into Ford's SUV and hightailed it down Kagel Canyon. A staging area had been set up at a school. Evacuees had been gathered there.

Paramedics had bandaged our hands. Fortunately, the damage was minimal. We asked where the two injured men had been taken. No one could help us. I was going to have to call Brenda, Mike's wife. I also needed to get his SUV back to his house.

I pulled a beer from my mini-fridge and handed Reggie another can of soda. The commercials ended and a local female anchor came back on.

"Wildfires north of Los Angeles in Kagel Canyon continued to burn during the night. Our Stan Fuller is at the scene. Stan, what's the latest?"

A young man in shirtsleeves and tie askew stood on the road leading up to the Boylston's house. "Monica, the good news is that firefighters have finally gotten a handle on the blaze that swept through this canyon yesterday and most of the night. Fortunately, there was little damage to homes. However, while attempting to quell the fire," the reporter said, "crews discovered the body of an elderly woman, the apparent victim of a gunshot." The camera began to pan back and he gestured to his right. "The dead woman was found in this house. Her identity is being withheld, pending notification of next of kin."

As the camera pulled back to a wider shot Reggie pointed. "Eddie, look, there's the Boylston house. That woman lived next door."

I remembered Helen Boylston telling me her neighbor Clara had called and told her about two young men with a brown van. "What do you bet ballistics will trace the bullet to that gun of Morrison's?"

"Nah, not taking that bet."

We finished our pizza as the news continued. After they wrapped up, I drove Reggie to his motel and told him to get in touch in the morning. He thanked me once more for pulling him out of that gulley. This time he had to fight back tears. I punched him on the shoulder with my bandaged hand and told him to forget it.

I called Brenda and she told me Mike had been taken to Olive View-UCLA Medical Center up in Sylmar. She'd been informed he was stable. When I phoned the hospital, an officious woman told me next to nothing. Only immediate family could visit. She also revealed nothing about Jimmy Whitmore's condition.

The events of the day made me feel like I'd been in the ring with Hulk Hogan. I hit the sack and dreamt of screams and burning trees. At one point, the Hulkster appeared as a fireman, threw me over his shoulder and carried me away.

***

Three days later I sat in Boardner's, a tucked-away Hollywood landmark on Cherokee, just south of the Boulevard. Early owners claimed this watering hole was the last bar in which Elizabeth Short drank before walking out the door to become the Black Dahlia. Another in a long line of urban legends that was ultimately debunked.

Over the last couple of days Reggie and I had, in firefighting parlance, mopped up. We'd given statements to both Pasadena and Los Angeles cops, as well as the FBI. I'd told them of the letter Whitmore had read to us, and Morrison's threats to kill Ford and me.

I sat in a red, cracked-vinyl booth awaiting Charlie Rivers. A few regulars slouched at the bar, nursing afternoon pick-me-ups. Charlie walked in, stopped for a minute to let his eyes adjust to the light and walked toward me. His armpits were stained with perspiration and a sheen covered his forehead. He squeezed himself into the booth across from me.

"Weather Channel says there's a chance of rain."

"What the hell have they been smoking?" I said.

"You got me." A waitress who looked like she needed a day off shuffled over and he ordered a bottle of beer. I pointed to my bourbon and nodded. Charlie said, "Thought you might like to know. That Jimmy Whitmore character was released this morning."

"To the hospital ward?"

"Nope. He's going home. He posted bail."

"What? When I talked to him he gave me the impression he didn't have a pot to piss in."

"Yeah, well, he's been patched up and is out of Olive View."

The waitress came back with my drink and a sweaty bottle of Bud and an empty glass.

"Who posted the bail?"

Charlie poured from the bottle and said, "You ready for this? Mike Ford."

I stared at him, unsure I'd heard correctly. "Are you kidding me?"

"I wish." He took a swallow and pulled a small notebook from his shirt pocket. "In your statement you said Whitmore had a letter implicating Ford in a rape up in Barstow. Is that right?"

"Yeah. It was from some Hispanic woman. I forget the name."

"We interviewed Whitmore and he didn't say anything about a letter."

"That's crazy. He had it in his shirt pocket."

"No trace of it, Eddie."

I sipped some bourbon and ran over the scene in my

head. I distinctly remembered Whitmore tapping the letter in his shirt pocket when he was lying on the floor of the Boylston house.

"He said they were using the letter to blackmail Ford into getting him and Morrison work in the business."

"Not what he told us. Whitmore said it was Morrison's idea to snatch the girl. They were going to use the kidnapping as leverage against Ford. No mention of a letter."

"What did Ford say?"

"He didn't know anything about a letter either."

"What did he say about posting the bail?"

"Nobody's talked to him about that. It just happened this morning."

The front door opened and a burst of sunlight filled the bar. I swallowed some whiskey and leaned across the table. "Whitmore's lying, Charlie. Someone got to him."

"Who? Ford? Besides you and the little girl, nobody else was in the room." He tilted up his glass of beer and took a healthy pull. "What are you implying, Eddie? Ford bought Whitmore's silence by posting bail?"

"Looks like it, doesn't it?"

Charlie pulled a handkerchief from his pocket and wiped the sweat off his forehead. "Maybe so."

"What do you mean, 'maybe so?' You think I'm just making this up?"

"Hell no. But I hate to say it, Eddie. It's their word against yours. Ford's kid isn't going to be a reliable witness. The only other person in the room was Morrison, and he's dead."

Charlie was right. Morrison was dead, but he wasn't the only other person who had been in that room in the Boylston house.

Frank Hughes, a firefighter, had also been there.

Chapter Forty-Two

As I drove up Kagel Canyon Road the scene reminded me of some sci-fi disaster movie set. I didn't notice significant structural damage to homes, but vegetation had taken a hit. Remnants of trees looked like toothpicks that had been dunked in an inkwell. To my right I saw patches of charred grass and crinkled shrubs.

Mavis had done her usual wizardry with the telephone and computer and had located where Frank Hughes could be found. Fire Station 74 was on Dexter Park Road. Across the street mud filled the ditch at the bottom of a steep incline that had been eroded by water from fire hoses. The firehouse itself and surrounding trees had escaped the flames.

I parked my car next to a dumpster and walked to the office. The heat was still intense. A wooden picnic table sat on a slab of concrete in front of the building. An Hispanic woman wearing a dark blue uniform shirt sat behind a receptionist's counter. She clicked keys on a computer and looked up when I approached.

"May I help you, sir?"

I flipped open my license and said, "Yes, I'm Eddie Collins. I called earlier? Wondering if I could speak to Frank Hughes?"

"Right." She picked up a phone, pressed a button. "He's on his way, Mr. Collins."

I nodded and sat in a chair by the front door. After a minute or two Frank Hughes appeared outside by the picnic table. He gestured to me and I joined him. He was smaller than I remembered, but of course he'd been buried under heavy clothing. Now he wore steel-toed boots, over-sized trousers held up by wide suspenders and a t-shirt with "Los Angeles Co. Fire Department" displayed on it. His hair was blond, short, and his face was deeply tanned.

"Thanks for your time," I said, extending my bandaged hand.

He looked at the dressing and presented a clenched fist. We bumped knuckles and he said, "Probably better you don't put any pressure on that hand." I nodded and he continued, "Burns?"

I shook my head. "Nothing serious. Looks like things have settled down a bit."

"For the time being. But it's a bad time of year." He pointed to the picnic table and we straddled benches across from each other. I brought him back to that day in the Boylston house and he said he remembered.

"I hear the fire got the shooter," he said. I nodded and he continued, "Yeah, well, that's too bad I suppose, but can't say I'm broken up over it."

"The guy you were tending to, the one with the chest wound? You remember him referring to a letter?"

Hughes thought for a moment. "Yeah. I had to rip his shirt open. He took it out of his pocket before I did that. Like he didn't want to lose it."

"What did he do with it?"

"Well, I'm not sure. I had him put pressure on the wound and then I ducked outside to see where my help was. Things got pretty hectic. I remember when I came back, the guy with the leg wound, the one with the little girl?"

"Right. Mike Ford."

"He'd hobbled over and was talking to the guy, holding his hand."

"Did you see the letter, Frank?"

"Man, I don't remember. My guys came busting in after me and things got pretty chaotic. EMTs were right behind them, and they started in with all their procedures. They had things under control, so I went back outside."

"But you don't remember seeing that letter again?"

"No, sorry, I don't."

I thanked him, crawled into my car and made my way back down Kagel Canyon Road. I got on the Foothill Freeway and headed to Venice. If Whitmore's letter was as damning as it had sounded, I wondered what the hell he'd done with it.

***

The argument for living on the west side of the Los Angeles Basin again asserted itself as I got out of my car on Jimmy Whitmore's street. The temperature had dropped a good ten or fifteen degrees. As a seagull flew overhead, something else dropped. On the roof of my car. I wondered if the bird was providing an omen for how the rest of my day was going to go.

Whitmore's bent screen door still rattled when I knocked. After a moment the door swung open and he appeared. The right side of his chest and shoulder were bandaged and his arm was in a sling. Cigarette smoke wafted through the screen door.

"What do you want, Collins?"

"I need to talk to you. Mind if I come in?"

He stepped back and I pulled the screen open. The air was thick with cigarette smoke. Newspapers were piled on the coffee table and the television set was on. Whitmore shut it off and sat on a chair next to the table. I sank down onto the sofa.

"How's the shoulder?"

He lit another cigarette, struggling with the matches and only one good working hand.

"Sore as hell. You come out here to play doctor? What's on your mind, Collins?"

"I hear Mike Ford posted your bail?"

"You heard right."

"Why do you suppose he did that?"

"He's your friend. Why don't you ask him?"

He got up and pulled a bottle of beer from his refrigerator. I watched as he tried to open it. He obviously was right-handed. The sling and he weren't getting along.

"What happened to the letter, Jimmy?"

"What letter?"

"Look, you can play dumb all you want. It won't wash. I was in the room. The letter from the Hispanic woman up in Barstow. What did you do with it?"

"I don't know. When they dragged my ass out of there, the cops must have found it."

"Wrong answer. They don't know anything about it."

He tilted his beer bottle up and took a healthy swallow. "Look, Collins, when the paramedics came in there, all hell broke loose. Firemen were all over the place. It was pandemonium, man. I don't know what happened to the damn thing."

"You wouldn't by any chance have given it to Ford, would you? Did he promise you he'd post your bail? How about paying your hospital bill?"

"I got my own insurance."

"You told me you weren't working much, Jimmy. Enough to get your SAG coverage?"

"That's none of your goddamn business, Collins. And I think it's time you left. I'm feeling some pain here, and I ain't in the mood to listen to crap from you. Hal's dead, the girl's back with her dad, end of story."

"Except for you."

"What do you mean?"

"What happens to you when the DA indicts you?"

"I'll worry about it then." He walked to the door and pulled it open. "Now why don't you leave?"

I got to my feet and walked up to him. "Rosa Moreno. That's her name, isn't it, Jimmy? Maybe I'll take a drive up to Barstow, see if she remembers writing to you."

He shrugged and slammed the door after me. A more bold-faced lie I hadn't heard in quite some time. The question was, why? What had Mike said to him when they were alone together in that house, waiting for paramedics?

I unlocked my car and noticed another seagull had left me a present. My indignation paled in comparison to the reluctance I felt about the conversation I was going to have up on Nottingham Avenue.

Chapter Forty-Three

I rang the doorbell and stood in the sweltering heat watching a jogger trudge up the slope of Nottingham Avenue. I didn't know what the hell he was trying to prove. His cardiologist could probably get it out of him, if he lived to make an appointment. I was about to hit the bell again when Mike opened the door. The look on his face that told me I surprised him.

"Hey, Eddie, good to see you. Come on in."

He swung the door back and I stepped into the air conditioning. He was dressed in a tank top, shorts, and sandals. His right thigh was bandaged, and he carried a cane.

"Thought I'd drop by and see how the patient's doing."

"He's about a step and a half behind. Thanks for taking care of my car."

"No problem."

He pushed the door shut and hobbled down the hall to the rear of the house. "How about a cold beer?"

"I wouldn't say no."

We entered the kitchen. Mike laid his cane on the butcher block and pulled a pair of bottles from the refrigerator. He reached into a cupboard and grabbed two glasses. We sat on stools at the breakfast bar facing each other.

"How's the leg?"

"A little better each day. Stiff as hell, though."

"And Courtney?"

"She's doing pretty well. We've been taking her to some counseling. It seems to be working."

"Glad to hear it."

"Brenda's not going to let me forget it, though. That'll take some work."

He sipped from his glass and we sat in silence for a moment. I tried to read his face, but he wouldn't look at me.

Finally I said, "What happened to the letter Whitmore read to us, Mike?"

He reached for a napkin and took a swipe at a drop of moisture on the counter. "I don't know. The police must have taken it."

"Rivers told me there's no trace of it."

"So you've been to the cops?"

"FBI, LAPD, the whole nine yards."

"What did you tell them?"

"What I saw in that room."

He shrugged, still averting his eyes. "There was a whole lot of shit going on around that house, Eddie. It probably got lost."

"That's funny. Whitmore said the same thing."

He drank and stared at the floor. The low hum of the central air conditioning was the only sound in the room.

"Mike, look at me. I know you posted bail for Whitmore. Frank Hughes, the firefighter that was in the house with us? He said Whitmore had the letter in his shirt pocket. He left, then came back a few minutes later.

You were holding Whitmore's hand and the letter was gone. What the hell's going on here?"

He finally looked at me and said, "I don't know what you mean."

"Did Whitmore give you the letter?"

"No."

He picked up his cane and ran it through his hands. For a minute I wondered if he was going to hit me with it.

"Okay, let's try this one. Did you rape that woman up in Barstow?"

He lurched to his feet and whacked the counter with the cane. It shattered into two pieces. I jumped off my stool and backed up a couple of steps.

"Goddamit, Eddie! How can you say such a thing?" He bent over, picked up the broken halves of the cane and threw them onto the kitchen counter, then leaned on it, his shoulders hunched over.

After a moment I sat down again and said, "I need the truth, Mike."

He turned to face me. "Why the hell are you making an accusation like that? How many years have we known each other?" He limped back to the butcher block and sat, glaring at me. "That's a hell of thing to say."

"I can drive up to Barstow and find the woman."

"For God's sake, Eddie, it's water under the bridge. Whitmore was convicted. What's done is done."

The implication of those words roared through my head. I looked into his face, this friend of mine. What looked back at me were pain and loneliness.

"So he did the time for you? You repay him by posting

bail? I suppose you paid his hospital bill too. What's next, Mike? Sunday dinners? Pool parties? He gonna be working in your production company?"

Mike pulled his stool closer and leaned into me. "Remember when we came out here? Two snot-nosed young bucks from the Midwest, thinking we were going to be the next Newman and Redford?"

"Yeah, well, that never quite worked out. For me, at least."

"Then listen to me. I've got a good deal at Paramount. Parkwood has got a lot of irons in the fire. There's room for you, Eddie."

I stared at him for a long moment, watching a friendship crumble in front of me.

"I can't believe I heard you say that. Now you're trying to buy my silence? I was on the business end of Morrison's gun too. I actually thought he was going to pull the trigger." I pointed to the rear of the house. "Mike, your girlfriend was killed back there, for crissakes. After all the shit both of us have gone through the last few days, it boils down to just some fucking job?"

I got up, kicked the stool into a corner and headed down the hallway.

"Get yourself another toady."

I reached the front door and heard Mike's voice behind me. "Come on, Eddie. Think about it, for cryin' out loud."

I tried, but I couldn't make it work.

Chapter Forty-Four

Sitting by the Pacific Ocean isn't the best place to brood, but I'd been doing just that in my office and all over Hollywood for the past several days. When Helen Boylston called, I thought maybe a fresh ocean breeze would clear the cobwebs.

It didn't.

Helen had sounded distraught over the phone and wanted some company; Jack seemed oblivious to what had gone down in their Kagel Canyon house. So I drove out and filled them in on what had happened. The loss of Clara Jesperson hit Helen pretty hard. They'd been friends for almost two decades.

I'd known Mike Ford longer. After I'd stormed out of his house, I had trouble coming to grips with the fact that this friendship had blown up in front of me. But in a town where promises go by the wayside and relationships based on shifting sands are par for the course, common sense told me I should shrug it off and move on. I was trying, in my own inept way.

A couple of recent news articles didn't help. A story in yesterday's *Los Angeles Times* said the DA had declined to indict Jimmy Whitmore. Insufficient evidence. Coupled with sufficient lies, I thought. Adding insult to injury, *The Hollywood Reporter* ran an item saying Mike Ford's Parkwood Productions had inked a deal with Paramount to direct and star in *Fortune's Folly*. Among the cast was one Whit Baxter. Jimmy Whitmore's stage name.

So the lies had come full circle. Jimmy Whitmore and his letter had become a linchpin for employment. That was his and Morrison's purpose behind the kidnapping. It had worked, for him at least. Left behind was the murder of Janice Ebersole. Hal Morrison's death was almost like wiping the slate clean. I wondered if Mike felt that way. I wouldn't bet against it.

I sprawled on the same bench near the Santa Monica Pier where I had first spied Reggie. Bright sunshine and a soft breeze were doing their best to cheer me up. Helping them were a pair of deeply-tanned roller-skaters sailing by in front of me, wearing bikinis that were nothing more than three band aids and a worried look. I watched them glide north, golden tresses flowing behind.

I got up, stretched my back and sat down, hunched over, and looked at my hands clasped in front of me. The bandages had been removed, but some cuts and abrasions were still visible. I thought back to the events that led to the damage. Reggie crawling toward me, fear and panic filling his eyes. Mike Ford sitting on a sofa, his little girl's arms wrapped around him, as if her life depended on him. At that point, it did. That's why it was so difficult for me to grasp what this friend of mine had done a few minutes later. Earlier that day he'd persuaded me to withhold evidence because of the danger his daughter was in. I rubbed my hands and thought about my daughter. Kelly, the one I did not know, had not seen, and perhaps never would. Could I have the same concern Mike had told me he'd felt? I had no answer.

My reverie came to a halt, when out of the corner of my eye I caught sight of the homeless guy who'd initially given me Reggie's name. Tony, I think Reggie had called him. He ambled up to the adjacent bench and sank down on the far end of it. He rubbed the stubble on his face and glanced at me.

"Excuse me, sir, but you look familiar."

"Yeah, I bought you a couple of meals a few days back. I was the one looking for Tired Reggie."

"Bingo," he said. "Now I remember. The porkpie. That's a fine *chapeau*, sir."

"Thanks."

"Did you ever find Tired Reggie?"

"I did. He told me your name is Tony. That right?"

"You are correct, sir." He got up and moved to the other end of his bench. "Do you mind telling me where he is? I haven't seen him for a spell."

"I got him off the streets. Maybe I can get him a job."

"Well, bless your heart, sir. It couldn't happen to a nicer chap." He scratched his chin and looked out at the ocean.

"What about you, Tony?"

"How do you mean, sir?"

"Don't you want to get off the streets?"

"I debate the subject every day. However, I can't seem to come to a rational decision."

"Well, give it some more thought." I reached in my pocket and pulled out my money clip. "I don't think you can debate on an empty stomach, though."

"It does present difficulties."

I handed him a twenty. "Maybe this will help."

"My goodness, sir, you are a lifesaver." He pocketed the bill and stood up. "Tired Reggie is indeed fortunate to have a benefactor like yourself. My profound thanks, sir."

He walked in front of me and headed south. After a few paces, he turned back.

"Do me a favor, sir?"

"What's that?"

"Give Tired Reggie my regards when you see him. He was one of the few friends I have had in recent times."

"Will do."

Tony saluted and ambled down the sidewalk. I hoped he would continue to carry on that debate with himself.

***

Reggie stood in the middle of the apartment, his duffel bag at his feet. He turned around and I saw a look on his face like a kid getting his first bicycle. He took off his ball cap, ran his hand through his hair and walked into the bedroom.

"So, what do you think?" I said. "Is it going to work?"

He stuck his head back through the door. "You kiddin'? This is great. You sure it's okay?"

"Bernie says it's all yours."

Bernie was Bernie Feldman, an undertaker friend of mine who'd helped me out on a case a few years back. We were in an apartment above his funeral home. Bernie had a USC student staying here who'd taken a powder without telling him. He needed someone to take the guy's place, functioning as a sort of live-in security guard. The place was rent-free, and Bernie would pay Reggie a few bucks a week to keep an eye on the premises.

"And it's on a bus line," Reggie added. "You don't have to keep picking me up all the time."

That was the least of my problems.

"Look at it this way," I said. "At least it's quiet. Dead quiet."

He looked at me, and after a minute, a big grin broke out. "Oh, man." He tossed his cap at me and I caught it on the fly. "I was gettin' tired of that motel. Some guy next to me kept playing a saxophone all night."

"Well, don't be taking walks around this place without a flashlight. Never know who you might run into." He laughed and I tossed him his cap.

"This will give you a mailing address. Then we can work on getting you some kind of ID. Maybe even a driver's license."

"Then I'd have to get a car."

"That's the idea."

"I don't know about that."

"We'll cross that bridge when we get to it." I stepped into the little kitchenette and opened a few cupboard doors. "Looks like Bernie's made sure you've got plenty of dishes and pots and pans."

"I hope I can remember how to cook."

"I don't know if I can help you much in that department. But you're going to need some food. I saw a Ralph's down the street."

"Can't buy much until I get my first check."

"No problem. I'll spot you." He carried his duffle into

the bedroom.

"Why don't you wait with the unpacking until later?"

He came back into the living room. "Okay. We ready for the supermarket?"

"After a while. There's something else we have to do first."

"What?"

"Take in that movie I promised you a few days ago."

"Hey, neat. What should we see?"

He picked up his key off a table and we started for the door.

"Well, considering where you're living, maybe we better take in a zombie movie."

I glanced at him to see if he'd made the connection. He shook his head and locked the door behind him.

"Eddie, you gotta get new writers."

I laughed and popped him on the shoulder. We descended the stairs and climbed into my car parked in a driveway next to the funeral home.

For some reason I thought of Humphrey Bogart's last line to Claude Rains in *Casablanca*. I didn't know if it would mean anything to Reggie, but Bogie was right on the money when he said this could be the beginning of a beautiful friendship.